I0586238

YOUR GREATEST MISTAKE

All characters, places, creatures, and events in this book are fictitious and figments of the author's imagination.

Copyright © 2022 by H.l Jones

Hljonesauthor@hotmail.com

Editor: Brittany Lewis

Beta readers: Brittany Willetts, Julie Willetts, Felicity Vincent, Natalie Wood, Natalie Thompson

Cover designer: © 2022 by H.l Jones

Copyright © 2022 by H Jones

All rights reserved. No part of this book may be reproduced in any manner whatsoever without written permission except in the case of brief quotations embodied in critical articles and reviews.

First Printing, 2022

Warning

The contents of this story is not suitable for anyone under 18 years of age it contains, strong sex scenes, coarse language, rape, sex trafficking and other adult themes, please remember to store your adult books in a safe place.

Other titles by the author

YOUR GREATEST MISTAKE

H.L JONES

H.L. Jones

Contents

I

Chapter

My breath is stinging in my chest. I have to admit it has been a while since any man gave me the run around like this. Part of me is pissed off that it has come down to this and my calm resolve was thrown way out of the window, but there is also that part of me that hoped he would run, that had hoped this would get messy and I would end up getting to hunt. I'm not proud of it but I know that sick and twisted side of me is there no matter how much I fight it. It's always there. Maybe if I fell in love and had kids and settled down it might change me? I doubt that very much though, especially since I don't get a choice in who I marry and have kids with.

Once in a while I get the freedom to choose what skirt I'll chase and eventually fuck then leave. I've never had a serious relationship. My family would never allow it. I dated a few girls in high school then after a while just stopped talking to me or they upped and moved away.

I know my family had something to do with it once my high school girlfriend Willow disappeared. She was not the kind of girl that could be bought or threatened. She was pure and honest to a fault which I liked most about her.

When she disappeared, I stopped trying. I knew I was dooming any girl that wanted to be with me, a fate I wish I spared Willow and the others. This is my life, if that's what you want to call it.

I'm hiding on one of the lower floors of the River Lily Hotel in Italy. It's nice but I find it is too flashy for my taste. I can smell the man I'm after from his expensive cologne that stinks so bad it smells like he bathed in it.

I can't stand people who try to push their money in other people's faces. It really shits me, especially when I know how in debt the guy is compared to others but I'll be damned if we are one of them a moment longer.

"Come on, Alex. You really think all this hassle is worth a measly ten mil?"

"Oh, Blake, since we are being so formal, I have killed men for far less," I smile, launching out from behind the pillar catching him off guard and shooting him in the left leg.

His four guards come at me and try to protect their boss but they were too slow. I shoot my gun four more times, never wasting a bullet and always hitting my mark. They all go down easily. I hold my gun to Blake's head while the other four hold their injuries.

"You should have chosen the easy way," I say, beginning to put pressure on the trigger once more. That's all I need. Blake breaks just as I knew he would. I'm relieved I didn't have to kill anyone and then again but I'm disappointed at the same time.

Blake makes some calls, moving things around eventually wiring the money through. I don't care. He is most likely ruined now. I have what I came for so I leave without another word. I walk out the main doors and into my waiting town car.

It doesn't take long till I'm at the airfield and hopping into the awaiting private jet. My phone buzzes. I look at the name and see *Devil woman*. I sigh and answer on the third ring "How can I help you Bonney?"

I hear her sharp inhale at how I address her but she doesn't comment. That means she is up to something.

"How did it go?"

I roll my eyes knowing she can't see me, one of my few freedoms from this wretched family.

"I'm on my way home. How do you think it went? I'm obviously alive and you would have already seen the wire transfer, so this is nothing more than idle chit chat or you are up to something, as you loath chit chat I'm going with up to something," I say dryly

"Ouch, Alexander, it really hurts that you think so little of me," she says with her best sulk, I haven't heard./ in a while. Whatever this is about it is no small matter.

"Enough of this pointless drivel. What do you want? I have done the job asked of me. Do you have another?" I say a little harsher than I mean to but I'm starting to lose my patience.

"Oh, Alexander, I do wish you would be a little nicer to me. I am your mother after all."

I grit my teeth. "Whatever can I help you with Mother?" I ask, forcing a nice tone she knows all too well is as fake as her concern for me.

She huffs. "Okay, if you insist on just getting down to business there is something the family wants. Tomorrow evening you will marry the Bright family's only daughter. They are a very prestigious family and this will make our families the most powerful in the world. No one will be able to stand up to us. This is what we have always worked towards for the family. Victor Bright is over the moon to have you as a son. His having only one child, and a female at that, was a great disappointment until he found he could marry her off to you. This is just the thing we all need."

"Have you finished your ramble?" I ask as calmly as I can.

"How dare you! This is the future of the family. You knew this would happen someday and here it is, better than any other offer we ever thought we would get for you. You should be thanking your lucky stars to have such an opportunity!"

"Cut the shit. I'll do it. You can stop selling her to me. If I don't you will have me shot or tortured until I do what you want. Remember, I have been down this road before and I know where it leads. I'll marry your choice, fuck her and give you little grandbabies you can torture instead of me. Now make your arrangements and leave me alone."

I hang up the phone, not wanting to deal with this topic anymore. I know this will be my one and only chance to get away with talking to her like that because she needs me and I just gave her exactly what she wanted with no fight. She knows if she pulls me up on my shit right now the wedding will take much longer to get done.

The small feeling of freedom that moment just gave me makes the fact I just gave them my marriage bed seem a little easier to handle.

My phone buzzes again. This time I answer the moment I see the name, *Dad.*

"Hello Dad. Is everything okay?"

"Oh yes, I'm fine. I was just checking on you, that's all."

"Once again you had no idea what she was up to did you?"

"I'm sorry son. If this isn't what you want, I'll do everything I can to stop this."

"You and I know that since you got sick and mum took over for you, you're not getting it back. They will follow her to the grave now."

"My burden to bear for marrying fifteen years younger than me."

"Easy for you to say. I'm the one that has to deal with her. She leaves you alone as long as you have your books and new ones coming in. You have no care what's going on."

The line goes quiet for a moment.

"I'm sorry, Dad. That wasn't fair. I didn't mean it. I just wish you would get better. Things have not been the same since she took over for you."

"I know what you mean and I understand but even if I did get better, she has the men's loyalty now and she has youth and good looks to keep their loyalty. The only thing I care about is keeping enough power to keep you as safe as I can." His tone is sad.

"Dad, I honestly can say if it wasn't for you, I would have left long ago. I will do this one last thing and when I start working for my bride's father I will take the chance to get you out of that place and build you a library bigger than you could ever dream of."

I hear his mood lighten. "You think me so simple? A few books and I'm easily subdued?"

"So, you don't want me to come visit you next week with all the new top sellers?"

"You play a cruel game Alex," he says with amusement.

"I'm sure with how busy they will be keeping me I can skip next week no problem."

"You could but I know you won't miss the chance to come get your pants beat off in chess."

"Oh yes. I can't wait for you to beat me again," I laugh.

"Every day you try could be the day you finally earn the win." I can hear his smile through the phone.

"I'll be there next week. You and I both know I'll most likely need the escape from my soon to be wife."

"I'll do everything I can to be there."

"No, I would rather you keep your strength for when I can have you to myself. This event will be insane and you and I know I'll be tossed around so much I wont even get a chance to see you. This isn't even anything special. Just more family obligation."

"Okay then, I will enjoy stealing your time next week and watch the wedding from here. I know they can set something up for me."

"Perfect. I'll get Lyncon to come over asap to sort it for you."

"Sounds like a plan. I'll see you then. Good night son."

"Love you, Dad."

"Love you, too, Alex."

I end the call and sigh. My dad and my friends are all I have in this world that keep me going. I find it funny that the woman who brought me into this world can't wait to give me to someone else and yet my dad can't get enough time with me.

I fiddle with the chain around my neck that my dad gave me when I was thirteen. It belonged to his dad and he was given it by his dad when he was thirteen like a rite of passage. I shoot my head up.

"Argus?" I call to my pilot and bodyguard.

"Yes, sir?"

"We are not going home yet. By tonight I want to find the biggest party and crash it. This is my one night of freedom and I'll be making the most of it."

"Yes, sir. But won't the family be upset?"

"They are always upset. Tonight I don't care. They are getting all their dreams come true tomorrow night and I will be the one giving it to them. Until I walk down that aisle I can do as I please and they will say nothing."

Argus flies us to a private airstrip where a private jet awaits us. While in the process of moving from one to the other, I try to call my best friends to join me for my self-appointed bucks night.

I get irritated when none of them answer and the jet is already in the air. I know the next nine hours are going to suck. Little did I know Argus had a little surprise for me.

The giggles rouse me from my chair. I walk past the three rows of luxurious white leather chairs to the three beautiful women who are sitting on a luxurious bed that takes up the entire back end of the jet.

I have a vanilla blonde, a mocha brunette, and a sexy Hawaiian beauty with long, black hair and legs I can't wait to wrap around my head while I bury my face between her sumptuous thighs to that sweet sex that I know is dripping for me even now.

The next nine hours fly by far too quickly. The blonde is on all fours as I drive my cock into her plump ass. When Argus announces we are coming in to land, I think to myself, *I'm about to do the same.*

I know how Argus flies and I also know the strip we are landing on in the Caribbean is a rough one. Even knowing that, wild horses couldn't stop me from fucking her ass. With every drop and bump it makes the experience even more enjoyable as we descend from the mile high club.

I move my hips as I pump into her sweet ass. She moans as I touch that sweet spot. With each drop and bump of the jet, a touch down in every way, I hear the skids and the rough feel of the landing gear on the tarmac as I climax, pumping my hot seed into her ass. She screams my name as she reaches her own finish.

I take some time freshening up before I leave my three beauties on the jet, passed out and thoroughly fucked.

I try calling Zac Adam and Lyncon again but still get nothing. I sigh, sitting in the pilot's seat of the helicopter, Argus has arranged to take us to the yacht that I will be enjoying the rest of the night in. Argus raises an eyebrow at my choice of seats.

"Don't give me that face, Argus. I was taught by the best. You showed me everything I need to know and where I am going. I think it is best that Mother doesn't know you had any part of it."

"If I may interject, sir?"

"No," I say, cutting him off.

"Sir if you insist on flying then that is one thing. Your safety is another. That is my job," he says. I roll my eyes, knowing I won't get far with him fighting me and my time is ticking down quickly.

I release my seat belt and climb out as Argus jumps in, happy to win. Once again, we are in the air. The experience is completely different to flying in a jet. We each have a headset on to drown out a vast amount of the sound, and most importantly, so I can communicate with Argus.

The sun is only about twenty minutes from going down but the sun still illuminates the incredible crystal blue waters so clearly that you can see the bottom. We fly past buildings that line the beach along with palms and trees that bring this incredible piece of heaven to life.

Max is on the beach where we land waiting for me.

"I can't believe you're here!"

"Well, I remember you giving me an open invitation. It just worked out well that you were having this party on my way home."

"I hope you will be staying long enough to enjoy the night."

"Oh yes. I have until tomorrow night so let the party begin."

"Yes, now that's what I'm talking about!" He embraces me tightly.

When he releases, he directs me onto his yacht where I find the party is well on the way. Most of the women are wearing a pair of bikini bottoms and no top with some jewelled bling around their hips.

An African beauty stumbles past me, spilling her champagne all over a man three times the size of what could be classed as healthy. He seems less annoyed once he sees her. Almost immediately, his hands are on her ass as he's escorting her to the lower deck.

A red head with a fiery attitude struts towards me with a tray of drinks, flicking her hair seductively off her shoulder.

"Can I interest you in a cold beverage?"

Everything about her is screaming, *fuck me*. I take what looks like a bourbon from her tray and press the chilled glass to my lips.

Her lips part as she watches my Adams apple bob as I drink the glass empty. She licks her lips as I return the glass to her tray and take another.

"Can I interest you with anything else?" she asks, seductively pushing her full bare breasts out to me. My eyes drop to her breasts for a moment before I return my gaze to her brown eyes.

I knock back the glass faster, this time taking the tray from her hands and placing it on a nearby table. I grab her hand and pull her towards the lower deck where I know the rooms are, earning an approving giggle. Before I get to my room a few more girls follow us.

"Get up!"

A foot comes in contact with my thigh. "What the fuck!" I grumble.

"Get up. You only have six hours until you get married and you need four of those just to get back. This does not look good. Who are all these women?"

I pull my head up to see Adam, Zac, and Lyncon, my best and only friends. I grin wildly. "This is what you missed when you didn't answer ."I laugh rolling onto my stomach and slowly pulling myself off the floor.

"Oh, wow I can't believe I missed looking like shit and smelling close to it too," Adam says sniffing me. "You stink of bourbon."

"Hey man, speak for yourself. I'm jealous as hell," lyncon says, squatting down to peek under a blanket sprawled on the floor where he finds a sleeping brunet. "Fuck I'm so incredibly jealous," Lyncon sulks still checking out the gorgeous woman sprawled naked on my floor.

I look around the room and find at least five naked women strewn in different places. Zac looks them over and then at me. "What?" I ask, knowing full well what he's about to ask.

"Don't play dumb. You didn't fuck all of them, did you?"

I grin widely. "Sure did! Many times and they all look sated to me. That redhead over there took a hell of a lot more than the others, but I got her in the end," I say, showing off a little.

"You're getting married in six hours. How are you going to settle for only one woman if this is what you need for one night?"

"What are you talking about? I marry who they want, fuck her a few times and that's it. The rest of the time I do as I please. This marriage will finally give me the freedom I have always wanted. Once this is done they can't touch me anymore."

Adam scoffs, "Bonney will never let you go. We all know that. It will take a serious deal with the devil to make that happen."

"Not everyone has the chance to marry the one they love, Adam." My words hit him where I knew it would shutting him down. He is lucky enough to be engaged to his best friend Trinity.

With his devotion to his one and only he makes life hard for those of us that enjoy what we can, when we can.

A groan comes from somewhere behind the couch, a dirty blonde lifts her head up. "Alex?"

"Yes, I'm here. Go back to sleep," I tell her while doing up my belt. She drops her head and falls back to sleep.

"Wow! Looks like you really tuckered her out. Good thing I wasn't here. If she couldn't handle you she probably wouldn't have been able to handle a real man," Lyncon remarks with a grin.

I shake my head at his piss take and throw my shirt on as we go out the door.

If any other man talked to me the way these guys did they would be dead, but with Adam, Zac and Lyncon, I would die for them. I trust them with my life and they trust me with theirs, and together we are an unstoppable force no one has ever been able to defeat.

We have made a name for our family with the accomplishments we have conquered and families we have ruined to get the family to where it is today. One of the biggest and strongest in the world, every last bit of it has been built on our blood and sweat.

Like the good little guard dog, Argus is clean and pressed, standing right out my door. Ugh one of these days I would love to see this guy let his hair down and do something crazy.

Four hours later we are at the airport where my jag awaits me. As we approach, Adam pushes me to the passenger side. "I don't think so," he says, hopping into my driver's seat

"Now you're going to boss me around?"

"I don't boss you around. But I also take any chance to drive a car I'll never afford, " he says, giving me a wink. I smile knowing I can't be mad at that and I still have a killer hangover from last night. I'm sure he's noticed, not to mention he knows I'll kill him if he so much as scratches my car.

Adam has never been good with anyone. He has been that way for as long as I can remember. He was a very shy kid when we first met. His family moved in when his father began to work for mine and in less than a year after joining as my father's employee, his mother, father and baby sister were all run off the road and gunned down.

My family seemed to have forgotten about him and I let him stay with me. We have been like brothers ever since.

Lyncon is the light-hearted joker of the group, always up for a laugh and as loyal as they come. He joined my ranks a little over ten years ago when his teenage self got into a fight in one of my favourite clubs. I was only seventeen but I couldn't stop smiling when I saw him. They laid into him good and he never stopped smiling. It looked like a joke to him the whole time.

Zac was a surprise. He's not like either Adam who is serious or Lyncon who is a joker. Zac is reserved and smart. He's very level-headed and his senses are off the charts. He's quick and precise.

Zac came into my company around six years ago after he stole my watch from my breast pocket. It takes an incredible man to pull something like that on me and almost get away with it.

I wasn't even mad, more impressed than anything. After that, I offered him a job that would give him more money than he could imagine and get him off the streets. He agreed to take the job with me, and we have been together ever since.

Outside of these three men, I don't trust anyone else. We all have our own abilities and together we are the strongest force you could imagine.

2

Chapter

I'm here freshly showered, shaved, and ready to face my current torment and my future torment. Honestly my life is so out of my hands. I don't care anymore.

We drive up to the Harlen family mansion that looks more like a palace. Once I'm at the steps, a valet opens my door to let me out.

I walk up the stairs and follow the white roses, baby's breath, and white tulle sashes that line the stairs, halls and banisters.

I walk into my father's office and find the suit they obviously want me to wear. A hairdresser and beautician are waiting for me as well. I roll my eyes.

If it wasn't for the fact the blond had big tits in my face while plucking and grooming my eyebrows, I would have thrown them all out. My patience is running very thin nowadays.

She moves in again and I'm starting to get the feeling she is doing it on purpose. I lightly brush the back of my hand against her upper thigh and notice her shift her legs apart. I grin. She is inviting me to touch her.

I look in the mirror and see the brunet focused on her task, doing my hair perfectly. I take my chance, relishing the challenge, and slowly slide my hand up the blonde's dress, gliding my hand up her inner thigh, giving her ample opportunity to stop me. She doesn't. Instead, she separates her thighs more so I can get access to my goal easier.

I can feel her wetness already moistening her thighs the higher I go. I glide my hand higher, still undetected by the brunet and find my goal. Fuck yes, she isn't wearing panties. This makes things much easier and sexy as hell.

I run my rough fingers at her entrance and I feel her legs shake slightly. Besides that, she doesn't move or show any signs I am affecting her at all. I smile inside at the challenge to make this woman come all over my fingers while I finger fuck her into oblivion without the brunet noticing. This is going to be fun.

I slide my finger in slowly starting with one. Once I've breached her moist entrance I begin to move in and out of her with the slightest of movements so as not to be detected.

Her legs part a little more, giving me even more room to move, but still, she doesn't make a sound. In and out I slid my finger until I feel she is ready for another. She inhales slightly at the second finger but doesn't say anything.

Slowly I pick up more speed, pumping my fingers and rubbing against her clit with my palm as I finger fuck her. She tenses slightly and I know she is close. I slide a third finger into her, earning a whimper. That's it, that is her undoing. I feel her pussy convulse around my fingers and her legs buckle slightly. After she has come down I retrieve my hand and suck on my fingers as she looks at me with hooded blue eyes.

She looks at me as if I just gave her the best orgasm of her life with just my fingers and she is definitely thinking about what I could do with my cock. I grin a devilish grin, showing I'm only too happy to show her.

A knock at the door reminds us I am about to get married soon. I sigh as they finish the final touches and leave when they are done, I wash and dry my hands as I check myself in the mirror.

The suit is ivory, with a white shirt and ivory cravat at my throat.

So much white I feel like I'm going to throw up and this damn cravat choking me isn't helping the situation at all.

I hover a little while longer, knowing I'll have to face this nightmare eventually. I check myself one more time, sigh, and leave.

The grand ballroom that we almost never use, it's one of those things where we have one just to say we have one rooms, but today it is decked out for a grand wedding.

The room has far more people here than I expected. Honestly, I thought because of the arrangement that it would be small, just immediate family. My heart drops for a moment when I realize this is her family. The room is filled with wealthy, distinguished men, all with beautiful women at their sides that look way too good for them.

Fuck, I knew this was not going to be easy and I knew my bitch of a mother would feed me to the biggest, baddest, richest wolves she could get her greedy, power-hungry hands on.

Not showing anything on my face, I stride down the aisle, calmly and with as much perfection as I would fire a gun. Each man looks at me as if he would gladly put a bullet to my head if I fuck up.

They all seem happy with my performance. I stand and wait for the main event, my wife-to-be and her father.

The music starts and they all parade in, one after another, showcasing more children. These are much younger though. *Holy shit! How many of these people are there?* With all the kids down and off to their chairs, my bride-to-be walks down the aisle.

It makes me feel like a complete ass standing up here all by myself. I know I told dad not to come and now I regret it. But I know it's better for him this way and my friends were refused in. Bonney said they needed to do the security detail. It just makes me hate her even more.

The two massive double doors open and my bride-to-be appears. She is wearing a long, thick, white dress that dips at the chest elegantly. The long sleeves make it very modest. Around her waist is a thick ivory sash that ties around her small waist into a perfect bow at the back. Six flower girls hold her long, diamond-covered train as she glides towards me. With every flash of a camera the jewels sparkle all over the spectacular dress.

I hold my breath as she walks towards me, her veil too thick to see her face. *Great, this does not give me hope that she is at least slightly attractive. Why would my mother give me even a shred of something to look forward to?*

Her father kisses her covered forehead and places her hand in mine with the proudest beaming smile directed at me that I have ever seen. Before he leaves, he nods his head to me and I nod back in kind.

The ceremony goes by like white noise. I'm all alone with none of my friends in sight, which is obviously my punishment for talking to Bonney the way I did on the phone yesterday and not coming straight home after the job. I knew she wouldn't let me have even a small piece of comfort.

"I do." Her small and gentle words bring me back from my thoughts. When the wedding is over I lift her veil to kiss my bride.

It only takes me a moment to recover but in my assassin's eye, her dazzling beauty ensnares me far longer than I am comfortable with. I stare straight into her ever green eyes framed with the most vibrant fire red hair I have ever seen. I lean in and press a kiss to her soft, full lips.

Fuck, I could enjoy kissing her. Remembering we are being watched, I break the kiss, turning us to face our families as husband and wife.

We dance and dine in luxury, unlike I have ever seen before. My mother rules the room with perfection, stealing the attention away from my new bride and I. I am at least grateful for that but her incessant need to cram a venue to its bursting point is ridiculous.

I am discussing new business ideas with Mr. Nakamura when I hear a gasp and a glass break. I look up to see my mother, Bonney, apologising beautifully to Mr. Tanaka, Mr Nakamura's associate. I know it was a load of rubbish because I watched her go to the bathroom straight after, no doubt to scrub her hands.

Bonney is massively against anyone who is Asian, black or even ginger. She is the most racist person I know. Mr. Tanaka brushed her hand slightly causing her to jump and drop her glass, but her recovery was perfect.

Very few people know because she is so good at acting and she can bend any situation to her will with a ninety-eight percent rate of getting things her way.

We arrange to do the send-off. My wife and I are dressed and ready. We have not had a moment to talk to each other at all yet and I am looking forward to finding more out about her.

We go through the large double doors to the stairs that lead down to where I expect my waiting jag, but instead, I find a 1962 Ferrari 250 GTO. I freeze on the stairs. My new father-in-law, Victor Bright wraps his arm around my shoulder with a hearty laugh. It is the first moment I have had a chance to really look at the guy. He's well built for a man of his years.

Victor's features don't give away his age, a sure sign he takes good care of himself. His hair is short and black with grey dominating the sides. His features don't look like his daughter Loralie's, making me think she must take after her mother, who I haven't seen.

"This is my gift to my new son. This car is the dream car of dream cars, worth more than 50 million dollars with the last one known to break the record at selling for $52 million. A small token from me to say welcome to the family," he smiles proudly.

A small token? What the fuck have I gotten myself wrapped up into? I never dreamed they would be this rich. If this is just my welcome gift, I can only imagine what our wedding gift is. Especially for his one and only daughter.

I smile and show my gratitude as the perfect spokesman for our family, making them all deliriously happy with themselves. We walk past my new ridiculously expensive car and climb into a waiting limo.

3

Chapter

We sit in the back of the limo on opposite sides, not even looking at each other. The car ride is long and very awkward but eventually we get to our new house.

Fuck, I hate how big my family home is, but this one looks like they kicked a royal family out of here! It is a fucking palace! My stomach turns and I know these people are the biggest money I have ever known. These people would loan money to countries, hell they probably *own* countries. This is making me even more uneasy.

We pull up and our doors open. From the look on Lorelie's face she is seeing this for the first time too, and I think she is feeling the same intimidating feeling I am. That gives me the feeling this house is a show to everyone about this union.

I hold my hand out, giving her a smile, hoping it eases her as much as I hope it will ease me. She takes it with a weak smile in return.

It's the slightest of touches but I feel the electricity surge through us. She gives me a look that gives nothing away.

Argus opens the back door for us. We walk up the grand stone stairs to the massive, heavy wooden double doors. In the entrance, it is open with very minimal but elegant furnishings around the edges of the room and very expensive original paintings on the walls.

An older woman greets us, perfectly pressed and with a tight, grey high bun on her head. She bows and without word, turns, ushering us through the house straight to our room. Once in the massive room that could fit an entire four-by-four house in it, the lady that I believe runs the household gives us the rundown of facilities and her instructions from Lorelie's father for us to have our dinner brought up and us not to be disturbed.

From this point on, the employees here are to be only visible to us when asked specifically and there it is. This isn't our house, it is our prison. These employees are her father's and he controls everything, even us being locked in our room to consummate our marriage and give him an even bigger family no doubt.

Once the doors are closed and we are alone Lorelie begins to quietly undress. I turn around to give her privacy.

"Does my body displease you that much?" she quietly asks.

"What? No, we have only just met. I thought you would be more comfortable if we got to know each other first."

"We don't have that kind of luxury. Our families want a child from this union so that doesn't give us much time for modesty and idle chit chat." I turn to look at her, realizing she is just as trapped as I am.

My breath hitches a little when I see her standing there sexy as sin in a pure white lingerie set and her white, satin after-party dress pooled at her feet.

"Honestly I'm a man. I have a gorgeous woman half naked in front of me. I would gladly do my part with great ease, but my concern is with you," I tell her honestly.

"You're nothing like I had imagined you would be."

"That makes two of us then."

"I imagined the big, gun toting mad man with a blood fetish like all the other men my father deals with."

I let a light laugh escape me. "You might not have been far off that assumption."

She walks over to me, gliding across our bedroom floor in sexy pearl heels with perfect grace. Her hips sway seductively as her ass moves to taunt me with its perfect firmness. Her hourglass figure is framed by a delicate white lace corset displaying her large, full breasts deliciously. Her legs are caged by white patterned stockings held up by a garter belt that I would love nothing more than to fuck her in while I tear the rest from her perfect body.

I raise my hands to stop her as she reaches me. "Please wait a moment. I have been married off within less than 24 hours of being told and now I am being forced into having kids with someone I don't know. I need time with all this. Me and birth control are best friends. This is not easy for me to just dive into."

"Would it be easier if I was that blond hairdresser of yours? You didn't seem to have much trouble putting your hands on her."

I raise an eyebrow, wondering how the fuck she knows about that. The blond wouldn't have said anything, would she? Unless that brunet saw and reported back. Fuck, I'm getting sloppy.

Her tone is calm, not accusatory in any way, so I decided to go with the honest approach. "Touch? Fuck? Sure, I can do that, but kids, this is not easy for me. That blond goaded me to play and I did, my final moments as a free man. She never got my cock and if she did it would have been protected. You don't know my family."

"Your family? Have you been walking around with your eyes closed? You obviously don't know my family. If my father finds out you were doing the finger dance with that hairdresser, he will put a bullet in her head and I would not like to think of what he would do to you. Not to mention a child is what they want. You thought you were going to be free after all this? You're wrong. Both you and I are caged for life. I don't want to feed any child to them any more than you do, but at least with a child we have some say as its parents."

I look at the floor, soaking in all her words. I know they are true. I think I just needed the hope that one day I would finally be free, but freedom is only a fantasy I'll never have.

"I can't do this right now. I need a drink," I say abruptly walking past her. I open the bedroom door and walk out. I follow the large, polished, wood balcony that skirts the entire massive room that leads down a long, red-carpeted corridor. I overheard that old woman say it had over one hundred and fifty bedrooms. Who the fuck needs one hundred and fifty bedrooms?

I keep walking, hoping I will find a room with a bar or even a kitchen. Hell at this point I would love for one of those maps that say *you are here*. This place is so big I think they will send a search party for me soon.

I turn a corner and collide with Lorelie.

"What the hell!"

"You scared me to death," she bleats.

"Scared you? What are you doing out here anyway?"

"You have been gone over an hour and I was thirsty."

I sigh. *An hour lost? Yeah, I can see this place being a huge problem.*

That's when I notice the milk and the broken glass on the floor.

"You found the kitchen?" I ask.

"The kitchen? No, I found four kitchens and I am betting it probably has more."

Fuck that is insane! This house is insane!

I bend down to help with the glass as Lorelie cuts her finger. I grab her hand and stick her finger into her mouth quickly.

"All kitchens have first aid kits. At least they are supposed too," I say, leading her back in the direction she came from.

I turn the corner and realize I have no idea where to go now. "Where to? You lead the way."

Lorelie rolls her eyes, still sucking her finger which is sexy as fucking hell but she starts leading me down the corridor to the kitchen she just came from. As I thought there on the far wall is a massive, white, metal cabinet with the green first aid cross on it just as I expected.

I pick Lorelie up and sit her down on the countertop with ease. "It's only my finger. My legs are fine," she laughs.

"I like it better knowing you are in one place not moving about."

She rolls her eyes again. "Wow. I thought it was bad before. Now I have to be told how and where to sit and stand," she taunts.

"I didn't mean that and you know it," I say, placing a plaster over her finger that has already stopped bleeding, only to stop her putting it back in her mouth before I lose my mind. I give it a little squeeze, earning a swat.

"Ouch! You did that on purpose!"

I smile, "Maybe."

I stop abruptly as she wraps her legs around me, pulling me to her.

"You and I are prisoners here. The best thing for us, is to make the most of it. We just need to do what they want us to and I will do my best to give you every freedom I can as I'm sure you will do the same for me. Outside of fucking each other's brains out I don't expect you to know or care what I like or don't like," she purrs seductively, undoing my cravat.

I grab her hands, stopping them from pursuing the buttons of my shirt any further. Before I can say anything back, she is kissing me fiercely. Her tongue invades my mouth, expertly searching for mine, making my mind go completely blank. My cock is hard in an instant, the fucking traitor. Her mouth is talented, unlike any kiss I have ever had before.

My hands are on her, without checking with my brain. Before I know it, I am ripping open her thin white satin robe to find her in nothing but the white lace number I left her in, *Fuck.*

Her kisses grow hungrier. Her hands drive into my dark brown hair, as I do the same, fisting my hand in her long, thick, vibrant, red hair, tugging enough to deepen the kiss, earning me a sweet purr from her throat, spurring me on further.

My body instinctively takes over. My free hand glides down her perfectly sculpted curves to her even more perfect ass. My hand glides along her thigh and in between her legs that she quickly opens for me further, pressing her sex into my hand. My thumb trails along the thin lace soaked in her arousal. She moans deliciously into my mouth.

My thumb applies a tiny amount of pressure to the delicate material protecting her entrance, rubbing my fingers along her opening, teasing her swollen bud. She moans, pushing me further. I apply a little more pressure and the lace gives way. I sink two fingers in between her wet folds. She gasps into my mouth, still locked over hers, both fighting for breath but not willing to part for it.

Her sexy moans goad me on, my brain having no say with my actions anymore. I rip the material further so there is nothing between me and her clit. I thumb her bud as I insert a third finger into her. She breaks free from our kiss, moaning deeply.

"I want you... please," she begs. Loralie kisses me again. Before I can answer or protest, her hands release my hair to pull at my belt.

Her hands are quick and precise and my pants are open. My painfully hard cock is free before I realise it.

Loralie places me at her entrance while pulling at my hand to free it from her. Grinning against her lips, I remove her hand from my cock and push her back from my mouth, laying her on her back and spreading her wide on the kitchen counter.

"What are you...." she tries to yell. I withdraw my fingers quickly before diving my face between her legs, stopping her sentence. I am all for sex but I just have this thing with having the one thing I can do freely being commanded to me. So I decide to teach her a lesson in how I work.

"Oh baby, for that little stunt I'm going to give you it all, but not before I punish you," I say, before plunging my tongue into her wet pussy.

She moans loudly, trying to push my face from between her firm thighs. I throw her legs over my shoulders and secure them tightly on either side of my face, giving me even more access to her. She struggles a little more desperately, trying to take control again but she has no chance. My mouth is locked on her sweet sex as I drive my tongue deeper, twisting, dipping and licking her senseless.

Loralie arches her back on the counter, exploding her orgasm into my mouth with a whimper. I know how sensitive she is right now but that doesn't make me stop. I decide I am not letting her go until I feel her come around my tongue at least a dozen more times. If she can last, I'll treat her to my cock.

I dip, nip, and suck, making her moan and writhe beneath me. Her breathing quickens again. This time she rocks her hips, grinding her sex into my mouth, lost in her building pleasure. She makes me growl, vibrating her clit. My arms lock around her thighs tighter as I flick her bud, earning a sweet cry. Her legs shudder and tighten, pinning my head between her thighs. *Fuck.*

This woman has the strongest thighs I have ever encountered before in my life. Her orgasm rocks through her for quite a while. I am too worried my head will cave in to enjoy it. Finally, it subsides, loosening her grip slightly, giving me room to move again.

"No!" she screams, trying to push me away again. "I can't do another one like that, Alex. Please!" She begs.

"Only when I have truly loosened you up will I fuck you."

She looks at my rock-hard cock that is still hanging out of my pants and her eyes grow wide. I think she was too focused on her goal that she didn't pay attention to the size of me.

I am not bragging but I am big and nine times out of ten it is a huge pain in the ass. It takes a lot of work to get a girl ready for my size and sometimes I think it is more of a curse than something to brag about.

Lorelie swallows hard, taking in my size. " I'll be okay. I can handle it," she says with such confidence I would almost believe her.

I smile and flip her over, taking her by surprise. I throw her perfect ass in the air and rip at her lace panties, giving me complete access from behind. Once again I have my mouth on her, driving my tongue in between her tight walls.

This time with no way for her to resist me or crush my head, again and again, I pull an orgasm from her and after each one she begs for me.

I have never met a woman that took this much punishment. I am exhausted and seriously at my limit, as I pull another orgasm from her.

I disconnect from her, pulling her ass down from the kitchen stone top and drive my cock into her slick, well-prepared entrance without her needing to beg me again. I am a mad man. My dick is on a mission and not communicating with my brain.

Fuck, stop this! Fuck! She feels *so* damn good and tight as hell. Fuck, I can't give in, fuck! Her moans are so sexy. She screams my name as I drive into her, taking me completely, she comes again and I feel her tighten even more around my cock.

"Fuck!"

I come so fucking hard I feel like a fucking teenager. I empty my load in her and drop my weight on her back as I try to pull myself back together.

We are breathing so hard I am sure her breath is stinging in her throat as if she just ran a marathon. I manage to gather myself enough to get up off her. I am about to pull out when she stops me.

"Not yet."

I have no words. Who the fuck is this woman? I grab her legs, turning her to face me while I'm still inside her.

She gasps but composes herself quickly as she throws her arms around my shoulders to steady herself. I don't say anything. I just look into her emerald, green eyes as she silently looks back into mine.

There in those eyes is a challenge. She is telling me she is not so easy to take down and she is daring me to try.

I pull up her dressing gown and cover her as best as I can with me still inside her. I wrap her legs around my waist and I walk us back up the stairs and down the halls, fucking her against railings, hall tables, pillars and any walls along the way.

I have no idea how many things we have broken or how much noise we have made, or even how long I have been inside her anymore. All I know is, the house doesn't stir.

By the time I finally find our room, I am fucked, well and truly, but Loralie is still goading me and I refuse to show weakness. I will take her down so help me.

I flop onto the bed, pinning her between me and the bed. The relief it gives my tired legs is exquisite. Her legs stay tight and unyielding around my waist. I struggle to kick off my pants as Loralie rips my shirt open, tearing it from my body and discarding it to the floor while I rip at the lace holding her breasts prisoner. Her breasts fall through the rips I have made only supported by the straps around the edges.

I suck one of her breasts into my mouth while I squeeze the other with my free hand. She moans sweetly as I keep fucking her well into the early morning light.

4

Chapter

I don't know what time it is, but it's dark when I finally wake up. I have no idea when I fell asleep or who won. I hope it was me. When I look over to my side I see Loralie spent next to me.

I grin widely. *Winner!* I think to myself. It takes me a few moments in my stupid teenager mind before I realise she is the real winner. Loralie goaded me into fucking her without a condom and not only did I give it to her, but I did it all night. *Fuck.* I am so stupid.

I sit on the edge of the bed and I laugh at myself. I actually married a woman that got the better of me well and truly, and not only did she take me, but I have never had a night like that in my life.

I look down at Loralie. Her lingerie is nothing but a few straps now. The lace is nothing but a memory. Her fire-red hair is fanned on the pillow in that *'just fucked hair look'* I find sexy as hell.

When she wakes up, she is going to need food and something to drink. If she can walk after that I'll be impressed.

I make my way to the door and find a huge silver cart waiting outside. I push it into the bedroom and find it has everything you could imagine on it. Crystal glasses, sterling silver cutlery, and all the hot foods are all on heating pads keeping them at a perfect temperature.

The smell of the food must make Loralie stir. She groans slightly as she makes her way up. When she sees the food Loralie drags herself to the edge of the bed where I am sitting with the cart.

I put together a light plate with fruit, oats, yogurt and a glass of freshly squeezed orange juice, placing it in front of her along with the trolley's red rose.

I get a disapproving look when Loralie reaches past me to the plate I made for myself with bacon, eggs, toast, steak, mushrooms and hashbrowns.

I can't help but smile as I watch her devour the plate. I make another for myself in time for her to finish hers, ready for a top-up.

"How do you have a body like that with an impressive appetite that could kill a horse?" I ask before shoving a piece of steak in my mouth.

Loralie gives me the wickedest look with those emerald green eyes and my dick hardens. *Fuck,* my plate is knocked from my hands as she pounces on me. I hear the clatter as the plate hits the carpet and the contents scatter across the floor.

Instinctively I grab her hands pushing her back, "Oh, no you don't."

Her deliciously plump lips curl into a pout as she looks at me with big pleading eyes. "I know what you are doing. I am not going at it again ungloved."

"Why bother? I could already be pregnant from last night and our families want a child."

I take her hands that are trying to escape to my crutch. "I told you I am not ready and they will have to accept that. Pushing something like this so fast is too much. Just give me time."

"But last night you didn't mind," she goads in a seductive hum, rubbing up my thigh again.

I stop her hand once again. "I said no. If you have sex with me, it should be because you want to not because you feel obligated too."

How the hell is she so eager to go again? She is not like other girls I have been with that's for sure, I don't know what came over me last night but I'm sure as hell not going to let it happen again. At least that's what I keep telling myself.

Once we have filled up on breakfast I get a message from Adam. I take this chance to introduce Loralie to my friends and give her a good distraction.

I walk down to the car garage. The motion sensors pick up on our presence, lighting the entire garage that is larger than most car yards. There are six rows of cars that line the vast space that holds more than one hundred high end polished cars of all colours and makes.

I move around the garage looking for my jag but fail to find it. I send a message to my mother and Victor asking about its whereabouts.

While I wait, I see the Ferrari and decide to take it for a spin. The drive is fast and the exhilaration of the drive is incredible. It doesn't have the same comforts as my jag but it handles like a dream.

The sexy curves of the body work is a plus but I'm not a fan of how low it rides to the ground. Plus, it stands out with its vibrant, traditional, blazing red colour.

The car is small with only two seats, good for a couple but not good in a work situation. Not to mention, the boot has very little space to hold everything a man needs in my line of work.

We arrive at Adam's house. It's a nice little four-by-two home with the perfect white picket fence. He always seems to apologise for its size but I don't think he believes me when I tell him it feels more homely than my own.

Trinity walks out with her arms open wide, "Hey trouble! We didn't expect to hear from you so soon into your honeymoon."

"Well you have to take a breather once in a while," I say, giving a light laugh and a squeeze when she hugs me.

"He's trying to distract me." Loralie has no fear and is in complete control of herself when she greets my friends. We all walk through the house to the back area where we always sit. The gardens are beautiful. Trin takes great care in them.

Alex loves his grill and cooking for us all. Lucky for Trin because she can't cook to save her life. The only time she tried for a surprise was for Adam's birthday two years ago when she tried to make him a cake. She was so excited when we all tried it. It wasn't until our eyes began to water and her garden had all our heads in it that she decided she wouldn't try again.

"Okay, what is everyone up for?" I am dialing my phone and ordering all the pieces Alex needs to cook my favourite ribs. Honestly his food is the best I have ever tasted and his plum sauce rib racks are mouth-watering.

Alex only shakes his head with a knowing smile as I end the call. "Okay, let's get this party on the way," Adam says, clapping his hands together.

"You know the drill Alex. You want your ribs. I want your coleslaw and potato salad," I laugh, putting on my apron Adam bought just for when I come to cook with him.

Loralie sits down at the twelve seater glass table under the patio area. She looks amused watching Adam and I in the kitchen.

Trin plops in a chair next to her with a bottle of champagne and two tall glasses. "You look like you had no idea Alex was a wiz in the kitchen."

"I didn't. In all fairness, I don't know much about my husband at all. He's definitely not at all what I was expecting and the more I learn the more I'm grateful for that fact."

"Alex has this thing with making out he's a big bad wolf but you won't find many sweeter," Trin says, taking a swig of her glass.

My potatoes are ready and perfect. Adam's favourite potato salad is with chopped spring onions, bacon, and boiled eggs. The girls have a good giggle as I slap his hand as it tries to steal an egg from the bowl that I'm trying to take to the table.

He succeeds, running off like a dog would with a bone, earning even more laughter for the girls.

"Hey, looks like my favourite little house wives are in the kitchen again." Lyncon walks down the side of the house towards us who obviously skipped knocking on the door and taking the side gate. "Hey Trin," he says, wrapping her up in a big hug. "This must be our new sister-in-law." He holds out a hand to Loralie who takes his. Once in hand, he pulls her up into a hug like Trin, taking her a little by surprise.

"Sorry Loralie. We can't do much about him but if you feed him he will never go away."

Everyone has a good laugh as Lyncon rubs his belly in agreement.

I've placed all the light foods on the table and notice when I'm placing the coleslaw that Adam is digging into the potato salad again. "You are going to eat it all before anyone else gets any!" I say, chasing him with the metal serving spoon I brought out.

I've caught Adam and I am bringing him back in a head lock while I give him a high school noogie. "Ah you fucker! You're going to make me bald and then Trin won't want to marry me."

I laugh, letting him go. "Trin would marry you even after your last hair falls from your head."

Everyone looks up to see Zac walking through the back sliding doors. I smile, "Looks like everyone is here. Let's dig in."

We spend a wonderful day eating and getting to know Loralie better. She seems to fit in with very little effort. All the guys talk to her like they would Trin who seems really happy to finally have another girl to talk too instead of just us guys.

It's late before we leave and Loralie and Trin already have plans to meet up and plan the wedding together. I have made sure Loralie is well and truly drunk before I put her back in the car.

Although it was my plan to put her straight to bed the moment she is in the house she is wide awake and sober as a judge.

Fuck she is so much more than I imagined. Her lips are locked on mine and her hand has my cock captive. Her kisses are potent, sucking any other thought from my head.

There in the doorway our moans echo around the large dimly lit room. She presses me against the door and I hear it click behind me. Her dress is up and I loose all thought.

The entire day and night she has been with my friends bare and waiting. I growl, spinning her around so that her back is against the door. Her legs are locked around me and her hands make quick work of my belt and pants.

There in the doorway my ass is bare and my shirt is barely holding on at my elbows. Not wanting to be caught, I try to move towards the bedroom but Loralie doesn't seem to want to move yet, pulling me in and kissing me deeply.

My cock is so hard it hurts. One more kiss and she shifts sinking onto my cock. *Fuck I haven't prepared her.* She is unfazed as she grinds herself against me. The feel of her ungloved is so exquisite I couldn't imagine any other way ever again.

I have spent the last few days ducking Loralie. The moment she has me she manages to entrance and seduce me like our wedding night and once I got to Adam's I found I had lost so many days I never even noticed. Then that night she did it again.

She is insatiable. If it wasn't for the fact that she is trying to trick me into going ungloved again I would enjoy the pursuit. Her techniques are very talented and I have to hand it to her, she is very persistent. Another sexy thing I find irresistible.

I am technically on my honeymoon. I have been taken off duties for work and we have been literally locked down in the house since our little outing. Victor has guards at every entrance. They say it's for our protection but I know better. They just want us in here fucking our brains out and Loralie is trying desperately to accommodate that.

I find the library. It reminds me of my father's back home. I know with his love of books he would never leave this room if he saw it. I walk the vast space with over eighty feet worth of space to the roof that houses the most exquisite library I have ever encountered. In all this madness, this place makes me think of my dad, the only parent that ever showed any kindness, unlike my mother he's always been very loving.

It's strange that out of this massive palace I would find a place that would put me at ease, not because I love books because that isn't the case. I am not an avid reader by any means, but because my father is.

I have managed to avoid Loralie for this long. I figure if I stay away for a bit we can both cool off and maybe I can get my head on straight. I'm not having much luck with a traitorous cock that is almost constantly erect since our wedding night.

I decide to gather some food from a kitchen I found closest to the library and some linen from one of the bedrooms I pass on my way back to the library.

I climb one of the old fashioned, polished, wood staircases up as high as it will go to the top most balcony of the library. The view up here is insane. The smell of books has always been my favourite because of my dad. I'm a grown man who has killed countless men and yet the smell of books makes me feel safe.

I curl up in a far corner out of sight but positioned to see the double doors below. I place the pillow under my head and blanket over me.

I'm in a dark underground parking area. It smells damp, stale, and of fuel and rubber. Besides a light dripping from somewhere, it's silent.

I make my way round the shadows. It was small but I heard it marking his location. Quickly and silently I move towards the sound.

I hear his breathing getting heavier as I get nearer. He's right behind the wall I'm leaning against. I check my gun and bullets then round the corner, pouncing on him.

We tumble to the ground, my gun flying across the floor. I move to flip him off me but he has me pinned. I raise my hand, balling it into a fist ready to punch my way free, when a slight flicker of light lights up the dark underground for a brief moment.

"Alex, it's me." The soft sexy voice calls to me like a siren.

The sound stills me. Her hot breath warms my cold skin.

"Shhh baby. I'll make you feel so good," she breathes, soft and breathy.

Her hands are running down my body. The fabric of my pants is straining from my erection that is as hard as stone now.

Her hands travel down, undoing my button and zipper, freeing me. The moment I am free her hot mouth is on my cock. I suck in a sharp breath.

"Fuck," I hiss.

I feel her lips on my cock curl in a satisfied smile. Her mouth, hot and wet, pumps my length in long strides.

Each pump she takes me in deeper and deeper until I feel the nubbed flesh at the back of her throat.

"Jesus Christ!" I curse loudly.

Losing all thought as my cock is sucked so fiercely, I feel I'll go insane. She goes faster and faster, hitting that spot so deep. I'm so close to my orgasm building to that peak when she stops abruptly. I let out a breath I didn't realise I was holding in.

The loss of her touch is gut wrenching. I begin to move my hands around in the dark in hopes to find her again when her warm mouth devours my cock again.

The sudden sensation sends a shudder through me.

"Yes," I breathe.

I reach out, trying to find her but all I get is air. My hand falls to my pillow at my head, bunching the fabric in my fists as she sucks and licks my sensitive head.

Her forearms have my hips pinned, stopping me from bucking into her greedy mouth. I'm building again when she stops at that point again.

"NO!" my voice calls out hoarsely.

I breath in and out, catching my breath again. I feel her arms release my hips as she moves to straddle me.

It's unlike any fantasy I have ever dreamed of. She positions me at her entrance and plunges herself down on me, taking me into her to the root of my cock.

Oh my god! No woman has ever been able to do this to me. My length and width is too much for most women and I have exhausted myself readying a woman long before we have sex which has given me great stamina, but this violent act is carnal and raw. The feeling of her is divine. I pump my hips harder, lost in the moment, driving up to meet her reciprocating movements.

"Yes, yes, yes!" Her screams of pleasure rock through me. I feel her tighten around me, squeezing me.

I come so hard and so violently, emptying myself into her. We both breath heavily, trying to catch ourselves.

A light flashes past a high window again, lighting the room for a moment, and I see her again, her piercing green eyes, vibrant red hair, and triumphant grin.

She got me again.

5

Chapter

After a week of being together we got our first taste of how trapped we really were and how depraved our parents really are. I woke up one morning and Loralie wasn't there.

I looked for her all over but found nothing. Then a very tall, very wide man invited himself into my home. I recognised him as one of Victor's men, Michael. Obviously the honeymoon was over and I had to go back to work.

Loralie and I didn't see each other through the next three weeks and I was not allowed to know where she was. All Victor said was she was safe while I worked. I was not allowed to ask questions at all. Before I know it I'm coming home and I am being pounced on the moment I walk through the door.

"Loralie!" My voice is shocked by her sudden appearance. Where have you been?"

She smiles, stroking my face. "Don't waste our time with questions." Her mouth is on mine, devouring my lips.

Oh god, I missed this. I manage to gather my thoughts enough to realise my need to know what happened to her was more than my need to bed her right now.

She pouts, "Awe Alex, please can't we have some time together first then we do the talking thing?"

"No," I reply, pushing her hands back from my pants. I grab one of her hands, yanking her up the massive stairs to the wing that holds our room. I have not slept there since she left. It just doesn't feel right without her.

"Alex slow down," she giggles.

I stop mid-way up the stairs after her red heel gets caught on the red regal carpet lining the stairs. I release her hand, grabbing her waist and throwing her over my shoulder and abandoning her shoe.

Loralie giggles louder. "If you're that impatient to have me, I am fine here on the stairs," she goads.

Picking up my pace, I give her plump ass a playful smack, earning a delightful squeal.

We are close to our room now. I turn the corridor and find our door open, and everything is set up nicely with food, candles, and fresh silk sheets.

I put Loralie down at the door, taking in our room. "Did you do this?" I ask her.

She shakes her head. "No I didn't. Is it me or is this just going a little too far?"

I look at her. "Somehow this feels like we have been invaded. What a complete turn off."

"Yeah, they got the opposite reaction to what they were going for I think." She laughs infectiously, running into the room, pulling the blankets down forcing the rose petals to scatter to the floor.

I stand in the doorway watching as she destroys every romantic thing in the room they had set up. Loralie is bouncing on our super king bed, throwing pillows and petals to the floor.

The two towels made into swans arching their necks into a heart is quickly unravelled and the twelve dozen red roses scattered round the room are now being thrown off the balcony to the fountain below us.

When Loralie is content she walks over to the food cart, grabs the bottle of wine, and pops the cork.

I walk over in time for her to hand me a full thin glass. "We have a week together, cheers." She clicks her glass against mine.

"Why do you have to leave again next week?"

Loralie ignores my question, downing her glass. I look into her beautiful green eyes and realise I am not going to get answers from just asking her.

I walk away from Loralie seductively, removing my clothes. Her greedy eyes heat and I see her bite her lower lip. As much as it affects me, I ignore it, continuing my painfully slow removal of my clothes.

I make my way down to my underwear. Slowly I hook my thumbs on either side and glide them down my legs, putting my tight firm ass she loves so much on full display for her.

When I return to my upright position, I turn, showing my cock she loves even more. Her eyes grow heavier, devouring the sight of me naked in front of her, obviously fighting her obvious desire. I know she wants me. If I didn't before, the way she is eating me alive with her hungry look is more than enough now.

She has followed me into the massive bathroom that has multiple shower jets all over the long, white-tiled wall and all along the front is clear glass. I open the glass door, step into the massive luxury shower, and lock it behind me.

Loralie's eyes grow dark when she sees my wicked smile. She tries to open the door, but the thick glass won't budge.

I stand in the shower completely naked and turn the jets on. They all flow from all directions, hitting me, cascading down my bare skin. She watches as I run my hands down my nakedness, teasing her gloriously.

She undresses quickly, obviously trying to play her own game. This should be interesting. If she can't touch me or kiss me, I might have a fighting chance to win a round with her.

Loralie is completely naked. Her body is perfection, from the curve of her hips to supple breasts framed by her long wavy red locks.

She steps forward, pressing her breasts against the glass. As sexy as she is right now, I want answers and I will win this to get them.

Knowing it's not enough, she parts her legs, pressing her entire body in further. I show nothing on my face as I glide my hand from my hair down the length of my chest, along my toned stomach to my cock.

Her eyes heat, blazing with want as she watches me stroke my long length.

"Alex, please let me in. I'll help you," she coos, pressing a kiss to the glass and leaving a blood-red lipstick impression behind.

I say nothing, heating my gaze, as I stroke myself harder. She is losing her mind. Loralie's pleas are more desperate than seductress this time. I know she will lose it soon. I press my hand against the glass, supporting my weight. I fist my thick cock faster until I break eye contact with her, throwing my head back in orgasm.

When I pull my head back up I see Loralie on her knees driving her fingers between her legs. "Please Alex," her pleas are desperate and needy.

"Tell me what I want to know and I'll give you everything you want."

She pants, trying desperately to relieve herself. My hand is still on my erect penis. I start to move my hand again.

"No, please," she begs again. "I'll tell you please."

"Tell me first," I command.

Her hand falls to her side, releasing her sex. "Whenever I start to bleed, they take me away, test me and make sure I am not defective in any way. I am then given injections to raise my fertility. Then I am housed out of your way until you have finished your workload in the two weeks until I am fertile again and the danger of your missions have passed," her tone is low and soft.

Loralie runs her hand through her hair and I lose it. Quickly I unlock the door and grab for her, pinning her head in between my hands, filled with fury.

Her eyes widen in shock and fear. "I'm sorry Alex! I have no choice," her words are panicked.

Softly I rub my thumb across the temple of her left side, uncovering the pale bruise marking my wife. if it wasn't for the fact I know every inch of her, I might have missed it hidden in her red hair.

I rein in my anger enough to speak, "Who touched you?"

Loralie calms quickly. "Oh I fell from my horse." Her look seems genuine enough, but it still bugs me.

All week I don't touch her, no matter what she does. I made sure she got her pleasure but withheld my own. Something about that bruise really hurt me and as swiftly as it came, they were over. It was at this time I realised my work schedule really did revolve around her fertility.

Sick, sadistic fucks. Even prisoners get treated better than this, with the inevitable game being played over and over.

It's been a few months now and my workload is insane. The time I'm not with Loralie goes by in a blur of work but somehow I still find the time to miss her. I finally talked Bonney into letting me come to Japan. It was either this or I told her a bunch of Japanese men would come to her.

I know it's cruel to play on her fears but at this point I no longer care. Mr. Nakamura I would class as a good friend and I enjoy his company immensely.

He greets me with an enthusiastic bow and I give one in return. We both smile. "I am so happy you are finally here," he says, giving me a pat on the back.

"How could I not come when you pressed so hard how bad things were?"

"Yes, but I honestly never thought Bonney would let you come."

"I am sorry about her but I can't do much about her."

"How did you get her to let you come? I would have thought no less than the threat of an invasion," Mr. Tanaka laughs as he comes into the room.

"I'm ashamed to say you're not far off," I say, giving him a bow as he enters and does the same.

"What a shame. I would love nothing more than to show her how great we are."

I shutter a little. "You honestly don't have a thing for Bonney do you? Not only is she a horrible person but she can't even handle being touched by someone she considers beneath her. But in the next breath she will have her legs in the air for any other."

"What can I say? I'm a complicated man and I like what I like."

I shake my head as he hands me a small o-choko of sake.

"Lets get down to why you are here. Mr. Tanaka and myself have been dealing with someone poaching from us."

"That seems relatively straightforward. What does this have to do with me?"

"We seem to think..." Tanaka begins but is interrupted by Nakamura.

"Actually, I think it's better if you look into this yourself. I don't want you getting the wrong idea straight away."

I frown at this uncomfortable awkwardness between them. Something is definitely up. This seems too simple, only they are acting as if it's more a problem of it being personal.

Tanaka moves Infront of me with a laptop and a stack of documents. I lean forward and begin to go through it all.

It has taken me a few hours but everything says the same. I even cross reference it with my own records and it all says Bonney is behind all of this.

I look up at the two men who obviously respect me enough not to go over my head in retaliation or even think I had anything to do with this.

"I don't have access to fix this, but what seems strange is it's so obvious."

"We thought the same thing, so we left these open as dummies once we saw what was going on to give us time to figure out what to do." They look at each other.

"We think that it is an obvious attack to make us...."

"Retaliate and sever ties with me?"

"Yes, that is what we thought also. That is why we dealt with it the way we did," Nakamura says, raising his sake to his lips.

"I am so ashamed. You have been holding onto this for months. I'm also honoured by your actions and how you dealt with this for me. I don't know what to say."

Nakamura places his sake down and walks over to me, lifting my head up to look at him. "This is not your doing. We know that and you have done far more for us than the measly amounts taken from our banks. We also know Bonney. You look like you need a friend that won't bend to them and won't judge you for them."

I raise my head proudly, feeling so empowered by his words. A few moments ago I was shaking in horror at how far my family will go to control me even down to hurting someone I respect greatly.

I give him a bow and hope he feels every bit of respect I have in this moment for him. When I lift my head I see him smiling brightly, "Let us drink!"

We spend the next few days getting completely drunk while touring all over Japan. We went to Hokkaido, Osaka, Kyoto, Nagasaki, Fukuoka, and Hiroshima.

The temples were definitely one of my favourite pieces. I love the culture and the tradition. I also love how they keep so much ancient history alive. Mount Fuji was breathtaking and the cherry blossoms in their magnificent pink hues were my favourite. All I could think about was bringing Loralie here someday to experience it with me.

When we return to Tokyo I'm given a great honour to watch an amazing samurai demonstration show casing the Nakamura family sword style followed by geisha entertainment and exquisite food.

"Nakamura, if you keep this up I'll never leave," I say with a laugh.

"Harlen you and I both know keeping you is not a fight any of us is ready for but at least we can give you something good to look back on when times get rough, speaking of which I do see rough seas ahead of you."

"You have always been good with sensing these things. I wish I knew how you do it."

"It doesn't take a genius or a spiritual man to see trouble follows you."

My phone buzzes and we both go quiet, knowing the fun is over. On the third ring I answer.

"Why aren't you done over there yet?"

"I'm just finishing up now. I'll fly out first thing tomorrow."

"You have been over there far too long. What on earth could have been such a problem it took three days to deal with? Get out of that filthy place right now! The mere thought of you being there makes me want to shower."

Her clear disrespect snaps something in me. "I will return tomorrow, not a moment earlier and if I hear one more thing about this I'll be going to Victor who will not be happy to find that you have been stealing from a very important contributor and friend of the family. If you know what's best, you will return every yen or I promise Victor will come up with something far better than a group of angry Japanese men in your room."

She gasps but doesn't say anything.

"From your silence I'll take that as you will fix this right now and Nakamura and I won't bring this up in any way in the future."

The line goes silent but soon cuts off. I look at Nakamura.

"You didn't have to do that for us. I am completely aware of what you will most likely go through because of you doing that."

"Some battles are worth the fight. I never want something to ever come between me and a good friend. My life is lacking in a lot of basic pleasures but I do have good friends and a beautiful wife with as much fire in her blood as she does in her hair."

Nakamura's phone buzzes next to him notifying him all the money that was taken has now returned. "Look at that."

I smile and stand. "On that note I will be off tomorrow, and I refuse to leave without spending my last night in that incredible hot spring you have hear you have been teasing me with for years."

Nakamura gives a hearty laugh and inclines his head to me. With a wave of his hand a lovely girl in a Sakura blossom kimono rushes over to us bows and directs me to the spring. She brings sake and fresh towels and even offers to help me pre-wash before getting in which I graciously decline.

The following morning I am the freest and most relaxed I have felt in my life. One day I hope Loralie, Adam, Trin, Zac and Lyncon can join me. I think the only way something like this could be better is with having the people you care about sharing it with you.

Things go straight back to normal. Me at work with Victor and then trying to keep my wife with me instead of her being taken every time they don't want me fucking her.

No matter how hard I try to stay awake to stop them from taking her I fail. They are patient and even waited me out when I refused to go to sleep for five days. Eventually I fell asleep and Loralie was gone when I awoke.

To teach me a lesson for that she was gone the entire cycle and the next. When I finally got her back she wasn't as fun loving as before. Her smile was forced on our greeting and I noticed the slightest discoloration on her skin. I turn from Loralie and bolt for the door in fury but the large thick doors don't budge. I pound them furiously, but still no one comes and the door doesn't budge.

I feel Loralie's hand on my shoulder. Her eyes look at me, unable to hide the pain buried in them.

"Tell me," I hiss, resting my head against the polished wood doors.

She opens her mouth to talk.

"If you spout one more bullshit lie about your horse, I will lose it. I have been injured enough to know healed bruising when I see it," I warn.

I turn my head slightly to look at her, showing the seriousness in my grey eyes. She takes a deep breath, preparing herself. "You're right I didn't fall off my horse and I was going to lie again. Honestly the first day I go back I am beaten for failing to give you a child, and when we made things difficult I was punished for the entire week. I need the rest of the time to heal so you won't know, but they underestimate you."

My blood boils. If I don't give in and get her pregnant they will continue to punish her. I throw my hands in my hair, furious. They really have me by the balls, literally. I am trapped and I can't do a thing except try to get her pregnant.

So, I do the only thing I can do. I stop fighting and take her all week. When I know it is the final night I don't protest or make things harder. I just hold her in my arms and pray I have saved her another beating.

6

Chapter

Loralie and I have an insatiable chemistry. Even I couldn't deny that. It was easy to abstain without her because I was worked to exhaustion. Then I spent my week with Loralie taking my pleasure and hers, enjoying those fleeting moments.

I never thought there would be a moment in my life that I would be wishing I got a girl pregnant but here we are. Each time we meet I learn a little more about her, and the more I do, the harder it is to let her go. Knowing what she will face if we fail doesn't make it any easier. I am beginning to worry if I might be the one making things difficult for the possibility of a baby. I have been beaten, shot, stabbed and tortured in so many ways I never even thought of what that might mean to making a baby someday.

I am excited for this job to be over as my week with Loralie starts tonight. A bullet flies past me, bringing my thoughts back to my task at hand. Some asshole has just done a runner after shooting one of my men. Honestly he's one of Victor's men, and the idiot was not smart enough to know he made a mistake before it was too late. When we get back from this I'm firing his ass.

The only thing I have to be grateful for is that Victor has let me have Adam, Zac and Lyncon with me now, making my job so much easier to deal with. Victor won't let them in on most information, but they know what they need and Victor is learning how well we work together.

"After this drinks are on you," Lyncon says, loading his gun again at my side.

"Why is it always me?"

"Are you kidding? The shit we go through without knowing a damn thing about what is going on. I think we deserve more than a lousy drink." Lyncons's tone is mischievous and playful.

As much as we all know I'm always shouting everything after a job like this. I still play along to lighten the mood. I know full well they deserve anything I can give them just for staying by my side.

"You knew full well what you were getting into before you started."

"That may be so but everyone knows you can't break up the dream team."

"Are you both done? How about we get this done so you all can get to your drinks, and I can get back to my fiancée." Adam's tone is exasperated from our inability to take anything serious.

I sigh playfully and nod to Lyncon who knows the time for play is over. He moves off from my side as Zac and Adam do the same, setting up a pincer movement.

I am running down the docks. We are weaving in and out around and supplies are littering the dock, ready for whoever collects them.

Another bullet flies past and I duck behind a larger wooden crate. I know he's not alone as I hear more gunfire from both sides of me. After a few more shots it goes quiet and I have no doubt it is Lyncon and Zac who snatched the victory.

I hear a click behind me and freeze.

Bang!

I turn to see a man on the floor with blood oozing out of a bullet wound to the head and Adam towering over him, his gun raised.

"How the hell did you miss him?" Adam snaps. "Whatever is distracting you needs to be put away right now. Focus! You can't be my best man if you're dead." The moment he's finished chewing me out he moves off, checking some docked boats.

I shake my head, forcing myself to get it together. My head is so full of a conflicting war about having a baby in general, let alone bringing one into this lifestyle, but he's right, I can't be torturing myself about babies when I have to be alive to have one.

I see movement to my right. The man I'm after shoots out from the back end of a docked boat Adam is searching. I don't risk Adam getting fired at in such a close range so I move forward quickly and loud, distracting the man.

I hear the sound of a speed boat coming near. My eyes dart to the absent-minded occupants. As I see him try to jump onto it as it passes by, I raise my gun taking the chance, and fire.

Bang!

I see his body fall to the water.

Bang!

Bang!

Michael, Victor's right hand man, kills the two men in the speed boat.

"What the fuck?" I snap.

Those men were innocent. You could see it clearly. They had no idea he was jumping onto their boat."

"The moment you fired your gun you signed their death certificates and any others who are witnesses," he states casually.

It has been four months working with these people and I still can't get my head around how they work. I know bad men, I have done shitty things, but this is a level I have never seen before. I thought I was the devil before, now these guys make me look like a saint.

This asshole I just shot was pinching money from one of Victor's side projects, which means a business so bad it's underground.

Zac, Adam, and Lyncon are back without a scratch on them as I trusted would be the case. They all begin to walk towards me but suddenly they stop and begin to walk in the opposite direction. I turn to see what made them go.

A limo pulls up at the end of the dock and I see Victor get out, dressed to the nines as usual, in an expensive black tailored suit and matching overcoat sitting on his shoulders.

"Good job, my boy!" he laughs, puffing on a cigar. "Things have never been so smooth since you joined our team," he beams.

"I don't know how when Lerch over here keeps killing everyone," I say, indicating to Michael who doesn't seem fazed with my remark at all.

Victor laughs, slapping me on the back, "This is the big leagues, my boy. You will know there are no loose ends, everything has to be like clockwork."

We walk to the end of the pier where the body is being fished out of the water and thrown onto the speed boat that has been retrieved, while another man is dousing the boat in gasoline.

After everything is set up they push the boat out. It glides across the water as Victor turns and walks us back to the other end of the pier to the limo.

"I have complete faith in your abilities my son and with some time and the opportunity, I think you could be greater than I ever was."

I stop. "What do you mean by that?"

"Didn't your mother tell you? When I retire you will be taking over the business."

"What? No, she didn't. I thought one of your loyal men were being trained to take over for you."

He laughs a full-body laugh. "From the moment you were born you were promised to me, the one I would train to take my place, and now here you are, together at last."

I feel a cold chill take over me. This was not what I was promised. They were after a child to raise for the business, not me! I can't take all this in. I think it shows on my face because the next moment Victor turns, abruptly springing his gun on me. He smiles a cold, chilling smile as his dark brown hair is tousled gently by the night breeze.

"You're not getting cold feet, are you son?"

His icy, grey eyes freeze me in place. This man terrifies me to my very core unlike any other I have ever met. He demands respect and fear in a simple look.

Bang!

He fires the gun. I hear the bullet fire from the barrel and whiz straight past my ear.

BOOM! The boat explodes behind me and I feel the heat from the explosion prickle at the back of my neck.

"No sir," I reply, unflinching like the perfect good dog I have become.

"That's what I want to hear," he grins, returning the gun to the holster inside his coat and disappearing back into his limo.

I watch the limo leave as I realise this just got a whole load harder.

7

Chapter

The sun has come up and things are done for the night. I took the boys for drinks and a steak dinner at Graces, one of the best restraints in the city that stays open twenty-four hours a day for clientele like myself that work round the clock.

The limo Victor insists I use is pulling up to the grand staircase to the house. I don't see why I have so many cars if I can't use them.

The door opens. I'm getting out when I am greeted with party poppers and streamers in the face.

"What is going on?" I ask.

My mother is the first to explode, "Loralie is pregnant!"

I look at her, stunned. I don't know if I am excited or terrified. This is what they all wanted after all. This is a good thing, right? I have wanted this to save her. I know now she is pregnant they wouldn't dare lay a hand on her, right? I look for Loralie. It is the day she comes back for our week, but I don't see her.

"Where is Loralie?" I ask, still searching for her.

"Oh, Alex don't you mind about that. She needs check-ups and all those things. It is normal. What you need to focus on is the celebration we will be throwing here tonight."

I scowl at her. "I don't give a damn about parties. I want to see my wife!"

She ignores me completely, wrapped up in her party planning.

I don't know how the demon woman did it but the entire house is a full-blown party within the hour. I have finally made it around the room where Loralie is being manhandled by idiots talking to her flat stomach.

God, I hope they are drunk. It is going to be even worse if they are not and this is going to be a regular thing.

Loralie takes one look at me and makes a beeline for me but is intercepted. Fuck, this is getting ridiculous. Mr. Nakamura intercepts me at the same time.

"Good evening," I say, giving him a light bow as he does the same. I have always loved talking with Mr. Nakamura. He always exudes confidence, pride and power but he's always been kind and I find, very educational.

His English is perfect and he loves to talk about Japan and the differences between Japan and the rest of the world.

"One of these days you must come back to Japan. We would be honoured to have you again. We have had some issues I think your talents would solve for us."

"As always, it would be my honour, but I can't say when I will have a chance yet as I will be integrating us with my lovely new bride's family."

"I understand. These transitional times are most difficult."

"I will get onto it as soon as possible though and I'll make sure the best men for the job will be there."

His eyes shift to Bonney making her way through the crowd of people to me. "I better go. We will talk soon. Thank you for your time." He gives me a bow and I manage to give a nod before he's gone.

He has never said it but I get the feeling he knows Bonney hates being around him. I wouldn't say that he doesn't like her but I feel he doesn't go out of his way to make her feel uncomfortable, just another thing I respect him for.

"What did he want?"

"Just discussing a new job he wants us to handle."

"Ugh, filthy things all need a bomb dropped on them," Bonney says, stirring a toothpick with a green olive on the end around a glass or what smells like vodka.

I frown a little. "I happen to like Japan very much and I find the food, culture and people far more agreeable than the ones here."

Bonney shoots me a look. "Do as you please, but make sure the price is right. Also you won't be able to settle this one as you will be on your honeymoon. I'll talk to Victor about taking the job."

"No, thank you. I'll be the one to arrange someone else for the job."

"Do as you wish, as long as the money keeps coming in and you make sure Victor is kept happy. Do you understand me?"

"Yes."

Bonney walks off, disappearing into the crowd of people as I throw imaginary knives at the back of her head. An arm grabs me from behind, catching me off guard for only a moment before I realise it is Zac.

"Hey man, why are you not wasted? I would be if I knocked a chick up," he laughs, downing a crystal tumbler of what smells like bourbon.

Adam comes to my side with a glass in his hand too, which is strange because he's not one to drink. I'm just about to ask where Lyncon is when I hear his voice close by, giving the worst pick-up line that earns him a sharp slap.

I can't help but smile as I turn to see him walk over to us rubbing his face with a grin. I shake my head at him, my smirk still present.

"You totally deserved that one."

"What? She was looking for a seat. I was only offering her a suggestion."

"Your face is not a public seat."

"You're just jealous my dick is still able to visit different locations, whereas yours would most likely get cut off if it did," Lyncon chuckles, grabbing a drink from a passing waiter.

"She does just fine keeping my attention," I say casually.

Adam and Zac seem to be frozen in time. "Wait, you mean she keeps up with your deviant lifestyle?"

"I am not a deviant."

They all scoff into their drinks. "We know you man, you have never gone a day without at least two girls under you and that is only because you were on a chase down."

"Actually, it was four. You forget the air hostesses," Adam corrects, laughing into his glass.

"You assholes are supposed to be my best friends. This is not helping me."

"Sorry but out of all of us, none of us thought marriage and babies were this soon in any of our futures, least of all yours who fingerfucked a blond moments before getting married," Zac laughs, losing his footing and tumbling into me.

All three of them are leaning on me now, drunk and trying to suppress giggles like drunk teenagers.

I take one step backwards and they all fall to the floor in a huge tumble of laughs.

These are my friends, my best friends, and they are expressing themselves how I guess I wish I could, so I can't be mad only happy I have friends who are so in tune with me that this news affects them like this, as if they are drinking to get rid of the gnawing questions screaming to be asked.

Is this really happening? Am I going to be a good dad? Will I fuck up like my mother or be amazing like my father?

What happens next? That is the scariest question so far. Ever since I got married things have happened so fast I have not had a chance to catch my breath.

Work is getting harder. Home is now going to get harder too. When these things happen they usually happen in stages, at least that's what I thought.

I feel like it's my wedding day all over again. Everyone knows the details before me, they get my bride all the way up until the end and once again I'm the last to know and everyone has their fill of her before I am even allowed to see her or even get a chance to talk about the situation.

I look down at the pile at my feet that I call my friends and decide *Fuck it.* I grab a drink from a passing waiter but before I can down the glass of bourbon I see Bonney's sharp gaze on me, I lower the glass from my lips and return it to the waiters Stirling silver tray.

The party is coming to a close. Everyone is finally leaving. Zac and Lyncon already disappeared into one of the one hundred fifty bedrooms with some girls and Adam is being scolded by his fiancée Trinity.

"You almost never drink!"

"I think that entitles me to let loose once in a while don't you think?" his question is low, slurred, and playful as he reaches to boop her nose but misses, resulting in his falling to the floor.

I sigh, moving over to Trinity as she struggles to get him off the floor. "Need a hand?" I ask her, already grabbing Adam's arm, pulling him to his feet.

"Thank you, Alex. I'm not used to this side of him."

"In five years you haven't seen him drunk at all?"

"Not like this."

"Please don't be upset with him. We have been together for most of our lives. This is rare. I know they are all like this for me."

She looks at me, knowing exactly what I mean by that. I have no freedom to be upset or worried. I can't show I feel anything, and right now my friends are letting loose for me, and honestly, I needed it. I needed the distraction. I needed the laughs. I needed them and they gave me just that, and Trinity knows us well enough to know it too.

Even after the party I didn't get a chance to see Loralie. They took her to the hospital for tests to make sure the baby was healthy and that was it. As easy as that my wife is taken from me again.

Three weeks later I came home to find Loralie on my bed waiting for me.

"Hey."

The first word out of my wife's mouth after three weeks of being gone is 'hey'.

I don't reply. I just walk past her and begin to undress ready for bed.

"I know you're upset," she begins.

"Upset? No, upset would not even cover three weeks ago when I found out I was going to be a father. Upset would not even cover the fact no one let me have a moment with you to discuss *our* child. UPSET DOESN'T EVEN BEGIN TO COVER THIS!" I yell, losing my temper.

I take one look at her and I know this is not her fault. I know she tried to get a moment with me, and I know she is just as trapped as I am, if not more.

I sigh, "How are you and the baby?" I ask, bringing the tone back down.

"We are both strong and healthy."

I nod, not knowing what to say. Fuck! I had so much I wanted to say before and now that she is here none of it is coming forward.

"I can't stay long. I found a moment to get out and see you, so I took it."

My head flies up. "What is that supposed to mean?"

Her gaze drops to the floor, "Until this baby is born, I can't go anywhere or see anyone. I have been gone all this time to make sure the baby is really yours and I do nothing stupid to endanger the baby."

"What? That is insane! No! I won't stand for it!" My blood boils as I pace up and down the foot of the king size bed that dominates my room. Wait, our room. I look around and realise Loralie doesn't have anything here. Besides the few clothes hidden away behind the doors and in draws she has no sign she is even here.

She sees me scrunching my nose at the distasteful thought.

"What's wrong?" she asks.

"I just realised we have no photos or any of your interests showing you live here."

Loralie seems shocked by my dilemma. "I..."

She doesn't continue, simply lost for words. "Let them come. I am ready for a good fight. This is ridiculous. I can't keep living this way."

"You know how dangerous our families are. This won't end well for either of us if we prove to be difficult, but if we give them what they want we can at least have a chance to find a small amount of freedom."

Loralie is pleading with me not to do anything stupid.

A knock at my door startles us both. Casually I walk over and open it. Four men at my door. Two are Victor's and two are my mother's. Oh, this is not improving my mood at all.

"Sorry to disturb you but we are under instructions to take Mrs. Harlen back to her quarters." This man's tone cracks slightly when he speaks, giving away that I frighten this man. *Good.*

I take off my jacket, open the door and lean against the frame in my doorway lazily, all my guns still on me in their holsters on full display.

I see them all shift but don't move, not wanting to show weakness.

"Tell Victor and my mother if they want *my* wife, they will have to come themselves. Any other will get a bullet and I am not giving another warning."

I close the door in their faces and stay by the door, silent and unmoving. Just as I thought they left, the door bursts open with all four guns raised.

I don't even move from the wall.

Bang!

Bang!

Bang!

Bang!

All four men go down. I move closer to them, their dominant hands now useless at holding the pieces they once held. I move around them, kicking their guns out of reach.

"You had to know this was not going to go as you had hoped. Our parents put you up to this and I respect your positions, but I don't give second warnings. The next time you enter my room uninvited or raise a weapon to my wife or I, I *will* kill you, do I make myself clear?"

All men nurse their hands. They nod their heads and leave without even trying to retrieve their firearms.

I know they won't come back so I sit on the side of my bed and three minutes later as I expected, my phone goes off.

My mother's voice screams down the phone. She doesn't notice me place the phone on the bed and gather some clothes for Loralie and I. She is still yelling when I retrieve my wind-up watch and cash from my bed side drawer. She doesn't even notice me leave her rambling on the bed as I leave the house with Loralie.

8

Chapter

I didn't take any of my cars. I know they are all monitored so we jump the back fence where I know there is a dark spot in the security feed and quietly leave.

I manage to flag down a random lady who I offer $1,000 just to take us as far as she is going. As luck would have it she is going through the city.

I hold Loralie in my arms as we drive. The woman is in her mid-forties. She doesn't seem scared and doesn't ask any questions. She just drives. She seems to have something big weighing on her thoughts.

"This is as far as I can take you on this stretch. My sister's place is the next turn heading a few hours out to the country."

"That's a big drive. Why are you doing this trip so late?" I ask, my curiosity getting the better of me.

She is quiet for a long pause. "My sister was in a car accident, a truck driver fell asleep at the wheel and collided with her and two other cars killing all five occupants of the two other cars.

My sister survived barely but she lost her ten year old daughter. She asked me to come up and sort things out because her and her husband don't want to go back to that house without her," her voice is dripping with heartbreak.

"You can't handle it right now either, can you?" I state more than ask. She nods.

"Why go then?"

"I can't be selfish when they have to be hurting more than me. No one should ever outlive their kids and too loose one so young and pure is just cruel."

"Why are you telling us all this?" Loralie asks the woman.

"Honestly, I don't know."

"What are you doing with the house?" I ask her.

Her eyes meet mine in the revision mirror.

"I think it's just getting packed up for now. Honestly, I don't know. They seem to want it sold as soon as possible, but I think they need time before going off rashly."

"We might be able to help each other."

"I don't know if it's the loss, it could be a feeling, but I just feel like I can't see that house right now and it seems like you both need a place to hide out for a bit, am I wrong?"

She sees me raise an eyebrow in the mirror.

"I don't care from what and honestly if you steal everything in the house it won't matter. At this point I think it's one match from being set on fire with all the memories it holds, so if you need it take it."

She doesn't stop. She keeps driving as if knowing our decision without it being said. The city disappears and the streetlights get fewer and fewer. Before long we are in a very remote area that no longer has street lights or even sealed roads now.

After a few hours the woman slows and takes a turn onto a hidden driveway so overgrown it is easy to miss, then stops the car, her breathing quickening.

She can't do it. She won't make it to the house. I can see that clear as day.

I remove a large stack of bills from my bag and hand it to her. "We won't steal anything, but we will use it for a while. I hope you can give this to your sister and it will look like you cleared it enough to rent it out for a while until you decide whether you will sell it or burn it."

She smiles weakly. She eyes the stack of money that should give her comfort she doesn't have to face this yet. "Thank you."

The woman takes the money and we get out of the car. It is pitch black but my eyes adjust easily. She hands us a set of keys.

"The house is at the end of this driveway here. It is a long walk but you will see the house way before you reach it."

Without letting us ask another question she is reversing out and going back the way she came.

"Should we be worried about how that just happened?" Loralie asks.

"She was not lying I can tell you that much, and I think she was so relieved not to have to face this just yet. It must be new."

I take Loralie's hand and pick up our bags with the other and walk. The walk takes a good twenty minutes into the dark before there is a clearing in the thick trees gathered around and overhead. This place was built for secrecy. Just up ahead the trees thin out on both sides lining the rest of the way and at the end is a beautiful manor.

Loralie seems to be shocked. This is no were near as big as what we usually have, but it is still bigger than what any normal person would have. These people must have money. Blossom trees line the road beautifully, the dark only showing they are obviously out of season at the moment.

The sky overhead is dazzling with bright stars unaffected by light pollution. The night is comfortably warm with a light sweet breeze, softly scented with pine.

Once we get closer an arched tunnel of what smells like jasmine lines the rest of the pathway down to the manor.

At the end is an open driveway that goes in a loop with a fountain in the middle.

We both drag ourselves up the stairs to the double doors. I slide the key in and turn. The lock clicks, so I undo the next lock and open the door.

Lights turn on the moment the door opens, blinding us both. I don't have long to adjust before a beep triggers a warning I know only too well.

A fucking alarm! I am about to lose my shit and rip it from the wall when I notice a number on the key fob. I lift the plastic flap and reveal the small piece of paper with 2011. I put in the number and disengage the alarm.

I look at Loralie who looks just as relieved as I am. I drop the bags that I am grateful to release from my hand.

We close the door and walk into an open room that is quite grand. The set up on entry is a lot like the palace my mother calls a house. Although this is a fraction of the size, it is warm and welcoming.

Two staircases, one on either side, take up the most part of the receiving room. There is a door at the top landing and one directly underneath on the ground floor. Everything is beautifully symmetrical.

Loralie takes the lead disregarding the bottom door and going for the top landing door instead.

Loralie opens it once we get to the top and it opens up into a wide hallway lined with photos and side tables topped with little personal treasures. There is a bronzed baby foot and hand encased in glass boxes with small places on the front.

Just as she said this is a family home. The photos line the walls. It looks like it was a happy home filled with a lot of love and great memories.

The first photo is a family one that looks recent. There is a mother, father, young son of about eight and a ten-year-old daughter.

They look like a happy family. By this door is a hall table with small objects that look like trinkets from a family trip to what looks like Egypt. Under the table is a drawer and inside is a photo album. Sure enough it is filled with family photos of their trip to Egypt.

At every door down the hall is the same. As we go down the time-line gets older. The kids get younger until the very end where it began is a wedding photo of the couple. There is a bouquet, a ring pillow and a wedding cake topper and a marriage certificate that are sitting atop the table.

This is the first door Loralie opens. We walk inside to a huge four poster bed dominating the room. It looks like where their life started. The room is dusty and looks like it has not been used in years.

It is late and we are both tired, so I open the curtains to reveal large floor to ceiling windows that look out onto a massive lake that sparkles with the moon light as it dances across the water.

"Wow." I think it but Loralie says it. I stand in front of the window holding Loralie in my arms, just letting the view wash over us, this little hidden treasure wrapped in tragedy.

9

Chapter

Loralie is the first to stir as the morning sun begins to brighten the largely windowed room. She turns onto her back, nestling into my chest, looking out over the lake that is so close it looks like we could easily be on top of it.

She jumps a little when I run my hand down her arm. "Good morning." Her smile is soft and sleepy.

"Good morning, do you want to talk about what is giving you those worry lines?"

Loralie's smile fades, "I'm wondering what they will do when they find out what we have done."

I run my hand up and down her arm again in thought.

When you never have anything for yourself, it gets harder for things to be taken. My own wife is one of the things I am starting to take back. I thought this marriage would give me freedom, but it only took more from me.

"They can't hurt us if they can't find us," I say, giving her arm a little squeeze.

Even with my words hanging in the air I know we are facing the worst of the worst when it comes to our parents and together, I can't imagine how much worse it can be. I push the uninvited thought out. I suggest a picnic outdoors today since we have never had a time without being locked indoors.

We find the kitchen that ended up being the central door on the bottom floor when we first entered the house and to our luck, the cupboards are stocked to the gills with food. Loralie and I won't have to rear our heads from here for at least a month with what we find.

We find a cane basket in the pantry that is an impressive room of its own. We fill it with tinned fruit, crackers, cheese, jam, wine, and a few other things we find.

When I come out of the pantry with the full basket, Loralie greets me with a blanket. I hold my arm out to her and she takes it with a giggle at the gesture.

As grand as this place is I have to admit I like how much more modest it is in comparison to what we are used to.

The property is even more breathtaking in the day. The driveway looks so far now it's light and I find it hard to believe we walked it just last night.

The sun is warm and the lake is still. The water is so still it reflects the sky and the lake's surroundings like a mirror.

The closer we get to the lake the cooler the ground becomes. Loralie sets up the blanket and I put the basket down and quickly gather her in my arms. She squeals in delight.

Her eyes meet mine and she kisses me sweetly. Her kiss speaks to me on so many levels, telling me so many things. It's free and grateful. I kiss her back just as sweetly.

Loralie's kisses become hungrier turning into a plea, I grab her hand to stop her but she continues to kiss me. "SSSt." My words are muffled in her kiss.

I don't want this. Her kiss was honest and then something happened, and that sweetness was taken over by a carnal need, not an honest need for me but one disconnected and perfectly tailored.

I would enjoy it if it wasn't for the desire. I must know her better, not the person they tell her to be for me.

She persists, driving her hands into my hair, tugging enough to send a signal to my groin. Fuck. I have to stop this. An idea comes to me. I begin to walk as she continues.

I smile into the kiss causing her to pull her head back, panting, "What is it?"

My smile broadens. She bats my chest playfully, "What is it? Tell me."

I flick my eyes down without moving my head and her gaze follows. Loralie's face goes white, "Don't you dare! I mean it!"

I take another step and drop us into the cool water of the lake.

I emerge with Loralie still in my arms, but her legs are wrapped around me, clinging to my waist for dear life.

Her breathing is quick and panicked, "Alex please take me back!" Her words are frantic and pleading.

That's when it hits me. "You don't know how to swim do you?" Loralie's face goes from white to a shade of red that almost matches her hair. I can't help but smile, "I think this just became my favourite thing."

"Why? You like me frightened?"

"No, not at all. I just like having one place I might have a little control. You weave me under your spell so easily, it's nice to have you for a change under mine."

Her green eyes look at me as if searching my soul. It seems she found whatever she was looking for because she relaxes a little.

"Well, you now know I can't swim. I am less than perfect. Are you disappointed in me now?" Her question is small and hurts me, feeling like my character just got knifed.

I push my ego aside and realize we don't know much about each other besides what the other is like in bed, but even that I feel we are holding back a piece of ourselves. I know I am.

"I don't want programming. I want the real you. I like knowing you have something you are not perfect at but you can't see it as a weakness either. With a little time I know you will be great and then you will be back to perfect again, but I don't want perfect. I want real."

"Well, it isn't easy when we only get one week a month together."

"We have as much time as we choose to steal now. You are already pregnant, you shouldn't be trying to seduce me to have one anymore. That need is met. From this point on it should be because you want to."

Her eyes look distant as if thinking this through. "I don't know how to be any other way."

I smile. "It starts with us being honest with each other. Nothing matters outside our bubble. That is us. We don't share our bed with any other and that should be the same with ourselves."

Loralie leans into me and kisses me softly again. It speaks to me just like the one before, but this time she pulls back, a simple chased kiss of gratitude, that makes my heart skip.

The brief moment was so pure it took my breath away, stripping us both raw unlike any lack of clothing could do.

I move Loralie, frightening her a little when I remove her arms from me, holding her hands in front of me.

"Trust me, I won't let anything happen to you. Tread the water like I am."

Her head dips under the water enough to get a mouth full and I hold her up higher so her face is above the water. She doesn't panic, she just tries again. It takes a while but eventually she gets it.

The look on her face when she finally got it was so precious. I couldn't help the pride and joy spread across my face causing her to light up even more.

Our daily routine started with breakfast and a swim in the lake, followed by a picnic, and then we would return to the house and explore.

We are taking a walk through the orchard today because Loralie spotted something on the way back to the house.

Every day we are away from everyone the more we open up to each other I learn that Loralie is very playful by nature and loves to laugh. She lights up in a way I never expected, stripping another hard layer from my heart.

Her hand is in mine as she pulls me through the trees on her pursuit for what she saw. I take this chance to ask her a few questions. "Tell me something about yourself."

"Like what?" she laughs.

"Anything."

"You first."

"Okay. I can play the piano but I hate it. I hate tea and I am addicted to coffee. I love sweet things but I hate fruit. Pineapple makes me gag. I hate beans but love garlic mushrooms."

Loralie smiles, still pulling me. "The fact that you can play the piano excites me, and yet saddens me you would hate it so. I love tea and coffee makes me sick. I love fruit and hate any bitter fruit. I don't like sweets but I do love savory things. I hate mushrooms and love brussel sprouts. I am indifferent to beans." Her smile broadens with my own.

"I hate TV but like the occasional comedy movie."

"Is that all I get this round?" she giggles.

"I never got anything back about a musical instrument." She ignores my comment but replies.

"I honestly can't tell you about TV or movies. I don't ever remember getting to see any. I hate cars but love boats. I am frightened of the water but I love the creatures in it. I hate clowns but I'm not afraid of them."

Neither of us ask, we only tell. Before I get a chance to give her any more I hear a whining noise and sure enough, we come to a small clearing and see a beautiful Black Friesian horse.

Loralie is completely captivated by him and I can see why. Sixteen hands, elegant and powerful with feathered lower legs. In all my years I have never seen a more impressive specimen.

Loralie moves forward as he moves back from her. After a few tries I see the excitement begin to fade from her face. I step forward, taking the waist tie from Loralie's floral sundress.

I leave a confused Loralie behind me as I walk towards him without fear of spooking him as if we have done this a thousand times before. He doesn't move, he just watches me.

I tie the thin material and carefully place it over his head and pat his side when he lets me. I turn to Loralie and wait for her to join us.

"Okay, out of everything you have shared with me that has actually stunned me."

"Why?"

"It's just that everyone always says animals are very intuitive."

"What? You thought because I kill men for a living, animals would hate me?"

"Ahh... um... no not exactly."

I can't help but laugh. "Believe it or not when I was a boy, I dreamed of working with animals. I even wanted a zoo full of them."

"Hahaha. Oh my gosh. Thinking of you with a zoo is *so* not the image I could ever see you with. Stables, yes, loads of dogs, yes... now that I think of it, yeah actually, I guess I could see all of that. Why don't you have anything like that?"

Her eyes lower sadly, remembering who we are outside of this place, and she knows the answer without me saying anything.

We walk back to the house and find a big beautiful stable. It is empty of horses but when I open the gate he walks in as if it was home.

Then the thought occurs to me, "Do you think the woman we saw was coming out here to deal with the horse? That would explain why she was forcing herself to come up so soon after."

"He does seem at home here and it would explain a lot, leaving them out in the fields to graze on long stretches. He would be out of sorts not having people he knew coming to him."

We close the gate, and sure enough, we find photos of this very same horse with a little girl of various ages up to about the age of ten. On the far side of the stall is a glass cabinet filled with ribbons and dressage trophies.

Loralie runs her hands down the glass as tears trickle down her face, I am wrapping my arms around her before I know it.

He was hers and he will never see his little girl again. I never thought something so distant from us could affect me but seeing Loralie like this breaks me.

10

Chapter

Loralie and I have been wrapped up in our little bubble of happiness, even with Loralie's moods changing as fast as a wind changes direction, swiftly and without warning.

Loralie is loving the water more and more as she gains weight. Now that she is showing, and every day that I see her tummy grow, the thought our baby is in there dazzles me in a way I never expected.

Loralie is swimming on her own now and splashing me is her new thing now her hands are free.

Unfortunately, the water is beginning to get colder, and I doubt we will be swimming much longer. A cold breeze blows, and I see Loralie's lip begin to tremble.

"That's it, times up!" I say, gathering her in my arms and dragging her out of the water.

"No, I'm not ready to go yet."

"Your lips are going blue. It's getting too cold, and you have to take care of the baby too," I say, towelling her off as her teeth begin to chatter.

"I hate it when you use the baby against me."

I smile, rubbing her hair fiercely with the towel, earning me a giggle.

"It looks like a cold front is coming in. We need to pack up and get Prince in too."

Loralie gives me a pout but doesn't protest any more. Over the last few months she has not been pushy or forceful. This place has brought out a soft, free side of her. No one has come to the house, but Penny, the woman who brought us here, did call the house shortly after we found Prince in a panic.

We put her mind at ease when we told her he was fine and being well fed and enjoying all of our attention.

I did not mention the fact he enjoys our attention so much he breaks into the house on a regular occurrence just to be with us.

Loralie almost fell out of bed in hysterics one morning after the first time Prince tried joining us in bed. Needless to say, the beds in the first, second, and third rooms are all now broken.

We found a room that has a fireplace that we thought would be good now it's getting colder, and to our luck Prince likes the blankets we set up at the foot of the bed near the fireplace more than the bed.

During the day he loves being outside, but at night he is terrible to leave alone. The fire is burning in the lounge room fireplace as we watch old romance movies Loralie has become addicted to.

But the thing she loves the most is when I play the piano for her when she has trouble sleeping. Loralie has not been in the mood for sex and I haven't pushed her, although this baby putting a damper on her sexual appetite is making cold showers in winter hard to bear so now I go for a run with Prince.

Loralie is curled into me reading a book with a long pillow we got at the local store between her legs.

The bigger she gets the harder it is for her to get comfortable and with cravings hitting hard I know I'll be back at the store again before the week is out. We try to go as little as possible to keep our whereabouts secret.

Loralie moves a little and I feel something against my side as Loralie winces.

"What was that?"

Loralie laughs at my slight panic, pushing me back against the couch.

"That was the baby kicking." Her hand moves to mine as she places it at her side where it kicked her before.

The moment my hand is on her side a powerful kick forces its way into my palm. In that moment I am awestruck, completely taken with this incredible moment happening right now.

I look up into Loralie's dazzling eyes set against the breathtaking glow of her skin and I am undone. "You are incredible," is all I can say.

She takes a few breaths, trying to accept what I just said. She lowers her head sadly. "I'm not incredible, I'm just the lucky one to carry your baby." Her words are sad and low.

"How can you say that? Look at what you are doing. Every day you nourish our child, making it strong and healthy. This little being is in there right now listening to us all because of you. Even if you were not pregnant with our baby I would think you were amazing. You're smart, fun and challenging. You're beautiful and captivating. There is not a thing about you I would change, except your love for cream cheese. That stuff does nasty things to you."

Loralie swats me indignantly. "You try smelling like roses when you're pregnant and full of gas." I laugh a full body laugh that stills Loralie. "That's the first real laugh I have ever heard from you," she says in awe. "You say I'm amazing and I find it hard to hear, for I see true wonder every day I have you near. You are incredible with animals and people, you can play the piano like your hands were touched by an angel and you don't ever look at me like I was property or something to conquer. You're kind and patient and you make me feel safe and cared about in a way I have never known." Tears begin to fall down her cheeks.

Another hard layer of my heart is ripped away in that moment. My hands are on her face gently wiping her tears, making her cry even more.

I lean into her and kiss her tenderly. The act is the first I have initiated myself, which leaves her a little stunned. Not wanting this feeling to leave yet I lean in kissing her again. This time I hold onto it longer.

Loralie's hands move up around my shoulders as she turns herself around to straddle me. I break the kiss. "Wait I –." Her finger is on my mouth stopping my next words.

"I want to," her words are soft, seductive, and full of want.

Her lips are on mine again, stopping me from asking her if she is okay with it, or how she will be with my length and the baby inside her. She seems to understand my worries but doesn't want me to think about them.

Her hands pull at the buttons on my shirt, slowly separating the material from my body with slow, gentle movements.

I leave her on her mission, watching her work her way to the button and zipper to my jeans. I lift my hips, making it easier for her.

She glides my jeans down my legs, freeing my erection.

"I'm in my birthday suit and you are overdressed," I say, provoking her to strip for me.

Loralie moves her hands to the hem of her dress when she freezes. I know that look. I've seen it before. I move my hands to her thighs, straddling my hips and my cock gets harder.

"See what you do to me? You're so beautiful, Loralie." My words are honest and obviously what she needed.

Her hands continue their way up her body, freeing her gloriously full breasts. Since the baby they have gotten even bigger and none of her bras are comfortable anymore, which suits me well to watch but not so good for my cock.

She tries to move up awkwardly to remove her underwear seductively but looks embarrassed when she fumbles. I catch her gaze and make quick work of them, ripping the material at the sides. The act spurs her on, forgetting the embarrassment she just felt.

Her hands are trying to cover herself as she moves up my body. I grab her by the legs and force my way down the couch until I am so low my face is between her legs.

Loralie gasps as my mouth claims her sex, sucking at her folds until my tong finds her slit. I flick her tiny bud and feel it swell.

"Alex!" My name is honey on her lips.

My tongue invades her, dipping into her slit. She inhales sharply as she begins to squeeze her breasts. Fuck, that is *so* hot!

How can this magnificent woman not see what she does to me? How can she not see how beautiful and amazing she is?

Her eyes fall to mine as I suck her, my eyes telling her everything my mouth cannot. Her eyes don't leave mine as she comes on my tongue with a blissful moan of my name.

Before I have a chance to do it again as I have grown accustomed to, she pulls away from my face, placing my painfully hard erection at her entrance.

Our eyes are locked on each other as she sinks herself down on my length. The movement is slow and teasing, letting her take her control.

Once she sinks all the way down, taking me in completely, Loralie takes a moment to adjust. Once she is comfortable, she begins to move on top of me.

"You are so sexy on top of me right now. You're whole body on full display for me to enjoy, I love seeing you sink your perfect pussy onto my cock and ride it for your pleasure. I love watching your delicious breasts bounce with every move you make atop me, and I love that it's all mine. Every fucking glorious inch of you is mine," I growl my words through my teeth hoping she sees what she does to me.

"Yes, Alex, yes. Anything you will have of me is yours."

"Everything. I want everything. I want the good and the bad. I want your touch and I want your tears. I want your joy and I want your sorrows. I'm a greedy man. I can't have anything less of you."

I move my hips into her deeper as she rides me, our words to each other ripping down walls we have spent our lives putting up.

I pump my hips, meeting her as she crashes her body down on me, driving me deeper into her. "Fuck, you feel so good, squeezing me so tightly."

Loralie pants harder, moaning louder. "Alex.....Alex I love you!" One more drive and she comes hard, taking me along with her.

Loralie collapses on top of me, but her belly hinders her to do so comfortably. I move her to the side, laying her along the length of the couch as I get up and find a cloth to clean her up with.

She is so tired it doesn't take her long before she is asleep. I pull the blanket up over her and watch her.

She just said she loves me. Do I take that as she loves me or pretend it was never said in case it was just in the heat of our love making? Well that is what you would call what we just did right?

I have never had sex like that before, and looking at Loralie's face as she sleeps peacefully, it was the same for her.

I find it impossible to sleep and decide to go for a run with Prince. I get dressed and decide to go to the store to get Loralie a few things I know she will like for when she wakes. I leave her a note and go.

It doesn't take long to get to the small store. There is an old pub and a service station where they pump the fuel for you. It's old and quiet here, giving it a charm all its own. I get off Prince and tether him outside before going in.

The store has everything from stock and crop supplies to food and mechanical gear. I grab some salted crackers and chips I know she likes and some jelly she was asking for the last time I came here along with food for Prince and a few other things to get us through.

"Is this all I can get ya taday son?" he asks me warmly.

"Yes, thank you."

"I never see ya with a car."

"Prince and I like the exercise," I reply, loading up the saddle bag I brought.

"I am glad to see Prince so happy. There was a lot of talk of him getting put down."

I freeze. "Why would they do that?" My voice is more of a snip than I mean.

"Oh, son I never meant to offend. It's just with that little Lacey gone no one could get near him. No one could handle him like she could. They had a bond like no other, at least until you that is. He has taken to you like a newborn to its mother," his smile is bright and thankful.

"I'm sorry, the thought of anything happening to him just took me by surprise."

"That's all right my boy. I'm sure he feels the same way about you."

I give him a nod and a brief smile before I pay and leave. I have everything set up on Prince's back including the heavy sacks draped over each side of his saddle.

"With this kind of weight, I think I should walk us back," I say, giving him a rub down the length of his nose.

As we walk back, I stop when I see an old, tattered phone box with most of the red paint cracked and peeled off from the sun. I play with the reins in my hand as I play with the idea of seeing how my friends are doing. I know it's a risky move but the need to know overwhelms me.

I decide to give Adam a call. He's my oldest and dearest friend. The phone rings out. I sigh. It's probably for the best, right? I go to leave when I decide to try once more.

"Hello?" the voice croaks.

"Adam?"

"Alex?" his voice is lowered to a whisper.

"Yes, I just wanted to check in to see how you are all doing."

"It was a risky move calling. Everyone is losing their minds looking for you. I don't know how you fell of the face of the planet. We are all doing fine. Trin is getting ready for our wedding soon and you know Zac and Lyncon, everything is fun and games. You just keep your head down and stay safe."

My heart breaks. He's my best friend and I know when he's lying.

I hear noise in the background. "Adam, why are you in a hospital?"

The line goes quiet for a moment. "Adam! Damn it, answer me!" That's it. I hear him crack and I know he's crying. "Tell me Adam. What is going on?"

I hear him hiccup through sniffles. "It's Trin, she is in the hospital."

11

Chapter

"Trin was in a car accident two days ago. They put her into a coma in hopes of stabilizing her, but nothing is working." His voice is filled with pain and I know he's not doing well.

"I'll be there as soon as I can."

"No! You can't come back, no matter what. There is nothing you can do. Don't lose this chance, not even for me."

"I can't do that. You are my brother. I can't live in bliss, hiding forever while my best friend is suffering. I'll be there soon."

"NO!"

I cut him off before he can try to sway my decision. I put down the receiver as the news begins to wash over me. Even though I can't bring myself to believe it, I am already moving.

"What's wrong? You look like you have seen a ghost Alex."

"We have to go back now. Adam needs us."

"What do you mean Adam needs us? Alex, what is going on?"

"Something has happened to Trin."

Loralie's eyes grow wide "What happened? Tell me!"

"I don't know the details but we have to leave now."

Loralie doesn't argue anymore. I know Trin means the world to her but I feel bad that it's my best friend Adam I'm worried about.

Fuck the consequences. I know all hell will break loose when we return but it was a time I enjoyed for the first time in my life, and I won't regret it for a moment but right now that time is over and all I can think of is getting to Adam's side as soon as I can.

It didn't take long to get back, pack up and say goodbye to the only true happiness I ever had. The entire drive back was quiet, although not uncomfortable. It was a silence we both needed, obviously dealing with our inner struggles.

Even though it is 4am in the morning we go straight to the hospital and everyone is there waiting too. Adam sees me and loses it in a way I've never experienced before with him.

I wrap my arms around my closest and dearest friend, holding him as tight as I can, desperately reigning in my own emotions so I don't upset him further.

I need to be his strength right now. If he sees me lose it I know he will be worse off, so I keep the wounded demon buried deep within me and hold onto him with everything I have and be the strength for both of us.

"You came back."

"Of course I did."

"You idiot, you were finally free. No one could find you."

"I would go through hell for you. Coming to your side when you need me doesn't sound like much in comparison now does it?"

Adam pulls away slightly to look at me as if he is going to yell at me again, but he doesn't, obviously lost for words.

Not wanting to suffer this stretch of judging silence or my selfish need to have his pained face stop looking at mine, I pull him back to me and hug him again.

"I can't lose her, man. I can't. We are supposed to get married next month. She can't do this to me!"

I know in this moment how much he really does love her. Honestly,

I never thought it would go as far as it did, but that could be due to my dry approach to love, as I have never had much that was truly mine.

My time with Loralie alone these past months has shown me something new and exhilarating I am only now seeing, something Adam must have had every day with trin and that only breaks my heart more. I keep thinking if I hold him tight I can absorb some of his pain somehow, but I know I can't and that hurts even more.

Outside I'm composed but inside a small lost child is panicking, trying desperately to hold something like water in his hands and stop it from falling away.

I don't move away from him. I don't complain about the snot and tears soaking my shirt. I don't get all manly and pull away. I just stay right where he needs me.

Lyncon and Zac look exhausted but they haven't left his side either. This is us. We are brothers to the end. We all share in each other's pain and joy, failures and successes.

Lyncon stirs and his eyes flutter open. When he sees me he shoots up, jabbing a sleeping Zac in the side. He wakes in a start, his hand automatically going to the holster hidden under his jacket. He adjusts quick enough to realise and withdraw his hand. Instead, he jumps to his feet.

I don't let go of Adam. I feel him still gripping onto the front of my shirt with both hands, obviously not ready to leave me yet, so I don't move. I make eye contact with Lyncon and Zac and that's all.

Lyncon sees the pain I'm in. I know it. A little flicker of something flashes across his face. What is he up to? That look is one he gives when he's going to start something in a big way.

He wouldn't dare. I'll fucking kill him if he upsets Adam any further. My silent gaze follows him as he strides over to us, his pace quickening. I move to intercept him but he ducks under my hand. I have just swung out to stop him.

Adam is shocked by my abrupt movement, but I think Lyncon tackling him to the ground with a huge kiss on the mouth shocks him more. Although inappropriate, it is effective. His crying immediately stops.

"What the fuck man!" Adam pushes Lyncon off him with his hands and feet while Lyncon laughs.

"Awe, come on. You looked so cute all teary eyed. I couldn't resist"

Adam jumps to his feet and chases a run away Lyncon who is taunting Adam.

I would intervene but this time it feels a little better seeing Adam distracted from his pain even if it's just for a moment.

Zac comes over to me, his hands in his pockets. He stands at my side while Loralie, Zac and I watch Adam chase after Lyncon.

"You were free. We all found comfort when you finally got away from all of this."

I hear the disappointment in his voice, as if my freedom somehow freed them too in some small way.

"Are you that unhappy I came back?"

"I'm always happy to see you. God knows it's been dull as hell without you, but you have no idea how much we all wanted you to be free of all this shit. We are your friends. Why wouldn't we want that for you? I know you want that for us and you would support it if any of us had the chance."

I know what he means. I'm about to say as much when Zac Looks over to Loralie and sees how big she has gotten. He flashes a pained face at me and I know he's pissed we came back, bringing our unborn baby back into this hell.

I was so desperate to get back to Adam I didn't think everything through. I'm just about to say something to defend my actions even though we both know anything I come up with will be a load of shit.

I see the doctor come out and everyone stops and stands to attention, his look giving nothing away. In those few moments it feels like the whole world is in slow motion and the verdict takes forever.

It's those first few words that throw everything in fast forward, "I'm so sorry." The world loses all light. Adam has collapsed onto his knees, his face to the floor. Loralie is crying and Zac and Lyncon are as I am - stone statues.

I know when we each come out of this we will all go differently. Lyncon is the first, his face turns red and before I know it he is putting his fist through a hospital wall, swearing.

Zac stutters at the doctor, "N-n-n-no! This isn't true. You're lying. There has to be something you can do. Get back in there and do it."

The doctor has probably seen this all before and calmly waits for us to accept things in our own ways. I know he has more to say and as the only one keeping a cool head I approach him.

"We have done everything we can but we can't stop the bleeding. She is on a machine keeping her alive for now but it won't give you much longer if you want to say your goodbyes."

Taking this moment in hand Adam jumps to his feet and barrels into the room, not waiting for anyone to lead the way or give permission and no one stops him.

We all enter the room Loralie goes to Trin's hand that is not being held by Adam. She quietly sobs while Lyncon and Zac stand behind her. I move to the right side and stand behind Adam.

The room is emptied of all the doctors and nurses that were in here for the past forty-two hours. The only sounds are the beeps and pumps of the machines around.

Seeing Trin this way, attached to all these machines, bloody and cut up will haunt me long after I draw my last breath, and in this moment, I wish I had gotten more time to know her better.

The beep sounds long and unbreaking, that deadly heart-breaking sound that invokes tears to fall from all of us. The doctor walks in and switches all of the machines off, turns and leaves us alone, in our heart break.

12

Chapter

Loralie and I didn't even get to leave the hospital before a massive squad from both her family and mine are out the front waiting for us. I am at least grateful they waited outside and didn't make matters worse in the hospital.

I move in front of Loralie, making it clear we won't be separated this time without a fight. The back door of a large, blacked out limo opens and Victor steps out.

"Good to see you my boy. Finally come to your senses I see."

I don't move or remark, I just watch his reaction. So far, he doesn't seem at all as angry as I had imagined he would be. Somehow, I thought there would be bullets flying at our reunion.

The sound of another car door opening and closing doesn't make me take my eyes off Victor, even when I hear the shrill rants of my mother.

"How dare you! Do you have any idea what you have put me through? What you have put *us* through?"

Her voice gets louder and louder as she continues her rant. I feel Zac, Lyncon and Adam before I see them. The anger I feel from Adam is screaming through the air between us, feeding the volcano inside me.

"ENOUGH!" The words are lose before I can stop them and how

good they felt, clinging to this explosive feeling I let loose. I don't care right now. Fuck the consequences and fuck them. We are all very raw and this was a huge mistake on their part, and right now they are going to realise that.

"HOW DARE I? HOW DARE YOU! First you shove a bride at me and God willing I do find pleasure in her company, you then take *my* wife from me without a word or explanation after you find out *my* wife is pregnant with our child."

My mother tries to butt in, fury blazing across her defiant face, but I don't allow it. She will hear what I have to say even if I have to write it in my blood and shove it down her miserable sadistic throat.

"You will not speak till I am done!" I seethe in her face, shocking her with my audacity. Her eyes grow wide. She looks around her, waiting for someone to step in but no one moves. From the look of it Victor is letting this play out.

She steps back, obviously frightened. Happy with this, I continue. "After weeks of being apart we find our way together again and you don't think we will want to be alone for a while? I don't regret stealing time with *my* pregnant wife, and I certainly won't apologise taking a simple pleasure you have starved me of. Don't you dare speak to me of what you have been through. We have come back to say goodbye to someone we love dearly and I'll be damned if I will let you make this moment any worse. We will return home, but things will change. You will not separate Loralie and I, and I will not have you butting into my affairs any more. That was the deal you made with me, now isn't it Victor?" I say, turning my attention to him.

Victor smiles, "That was our deal indeed and you are right my boy. You have not done anything that any one of us would be entitled to. You are home, and you are both safe. I think we let things be."

My mother's face goes a violent shade of red, but one sharp look from Victor and she shuts down without a fight, storming off in a huff.

With one wave of Victor's hand the mass of people disperse until it is just the six of us. I don't move to thank him. I won't bow in gratitude for a simple freedom granted any normal man.

Victor casually walks to me and I don't move. It happens so fast I barely register it. He drops his coat off his shoulders and bolts at me, one almighty jab to the gut followed even faster by a swing to my jaw.

As fast as it happens, it is over. I manage to stay on my feet. I have no fucking idea how, but I do. For a seasoned man he is a fierce fighter. I would hate to go head to head with him in a serious fight.

I adjust myself, spit out a mouth full of blood and straighten myself as before.

Victor turns from me, collects his coat and swings it round to sit on his shoulders once again. Without a word he climbs into the limo as his driver closes the door after him and leaves.

The moment they are out of sight Loralie is at my side with the others. Her hands are on my face obviously seeing the damage Victor may have done.

"I'm fine. Don't worry." I wince a little when Lyncon pokes me in the stomach.

"Yeah, sure you are. That old man sure can pack a punch. It looks like you at least have a few cracked ribs, and God only knows what he did to your jaw."

Adam is standing in front of me, mouth open. "I can't believe it. I never thought I would ever see you stand up to your mother. Hell, I can't believe Victor shut her down like that!"

"Yeah, but I am very sure I won't hear the end of it, and I know I will still have the fall out for this, but right now in this moment I am just going to relish in it."

I put my hand to my rib cage, instinctively taking in shallow breaths. I am well adept with broken ribs, fuck knows I have had enough of them.

Victor showed me mercy. Fuck knows why, but I do know I am lucky to walk away with what I did.

Adam turns to the hospital doors at our back, obviously battling with the thought of having to go back in there for me.

I throw a free arm around Loralie and begin to walk away from the hospital.

"W-w-w-wait you need to see a doctor," Loralie stutters.

"Fuck that. I am not going back in there. If it will shut you all up, I will have the on-call doctor come out and see me. Now let's go."

"Where are we going? You just won a major battle."

I stop and look at Lyncon, Zac and Adam and we all smile.

"Oh, hell yes," Adam says in pure appreciation.

Loralie looks around at us trying to get in on the silent convocation she is being left out of. "What?"

We all laugh, "We are going somewhere you go when you want to escape the bad and find a laugh, no matter how bad. We are going home to Dad."

Loralie looks confused, "But what about your mum? Won't she be there?"

We all scoff. "Dad has been living in his family home since he got sick two years ago. Besides, when she rings him to gloat about something, she doesn't bother with him at all. She over ran the family home and effectively pushed him out so he retreated and she didn't care."

"Wow... and here I thought my father was cold."

I see Loralie is nervous the whole trip. I grab her hand, trying to calm her when I see her hands start to shake. "Don't worry. He won't bite," I say, giving her hand a squeeze as I press a kiss to her hand.

"I don't doubt he is kind. It's just that I know how much he means to you and I want him to like me."

I burst inside, a flood of feeling washing over me, stealing my words. So I just smile and give her a sweet, chased kiss, obviously calming her instantly.

"We are here," Lyncon calls from the front seat.

Adam is the first one bolting out the door. It breaks my heart. He's in so much pain. He's running to the only parent he has known, and as I get out of the black SUV, he's waiting on the top step, his arms open wide as Adam is the first to take their comfort.

We all take our time getting out of the car and making our way up the stairs to the massive old mansion. It is grander than the manor we just left but far more comfortable than the over-the-top palaces Victor, my mother and I lived in.

I never felt at home in any of those places but I have always felt at home here. Mother hates coming here. She says it's too old and outdated.

Dad gives me a welcoming smile. His eyes brighten even more when he sees Loralie, but at no time does he push Adam away, leaving him to take his fill.

We all know the drill in these times. God knows we have all taken Dad prisoner at one point or another and he treats us all the same.

We walk past and leave Dad to give Adam what he needs, the very reason we all thought to come in the first place. The main entrance is dark, lowly lit by a large crystal chandelier hanging in the centre of the room. I'll have to make a note to get that cleaned. It's so dusty it's barely giving off any light at all.

As we walk through the halls to the main lounge room, I notice it is very quiet and very dusty. Loralie gives me a concerned look.

"Doesn't he have people looking after him?"

Her question is the same as mine. Where is everyone? There should be chiefs and cleaners, servers, nurses, gardeners, but there is no one at all.

13

Chapter

Loralie and I are cleaning up the main lounge room when Dad and Adam finally come in. For as long as they took it seemed Adam really needed Dad. With how much better he looks, Dad obviously worked his magic once again.

He gives Loralie and I a disapproving look because of our cleaning escapade. "Don't give us that look. What is going on here?" I ask.

He sighs, "Your mother thought I had some part in your disappearance, so she removed everyone from the house. Honestly the house has never been more enjoyable." His hearty laugh and bright smile make it hard not to want to smile along with him.

But I find it hard to smile when his lack of help is due to Loralie and me. He notices and shuts my thought down. "Don't you think this is a bad thing. I have never been happier to have all her spies out of here. This place was my parents and theirs before them, back further than I can even imagine. This is where true peace is. I'll get things sorted. I have ways. Don't you worry about me. Now put those things down. Sit and tell me everything."

We all look at each other and know we will get around this fight a little later. Right now we need what we came for and Dad is pushing for that very thing. So we all let go, sit down, and tell him everything.

Adam is the first, followed by Zac and Lyncon who gives Dad the biggest laugh when he explains about Michael having to chase down a man on the run while I was away. With how Lerch is built, I find it hard to imagine him running at all, but with Lyncon's visual dramatics of a six foot robot running it was hard not to picture.

Zac and Lyncon keep going off to chop wood and feed the fire while Loralie and I kept the food and drinks coming.

The night has been wonderful despite the dark cloud looming at Trin's loss, we manage a bit of laughing and joking. It was great to hear everything that has happened while we have been gone.

Dad is the first to rise, "I'm sorry everyone. I'm no spring chicken anymore. I need to rest up now."

We all smile and rise.

"Do you need a hand?" My offer to help is instantly shut down.

"Don't you fuss over me now. I've been fine on my own these last few months and I'll be fine to continue on as I have done so." He moves over to Loralie and gives her a hug and a kiss to her forehead. "This magnificent treasure is what you should be fussing over." He takes a step back to look her over, taking in her little popped belly.

"Thank you so much." Loralie's eyes well up from the endearment my father is giving her.

"You're carrying my grandbaby and not only that, I have never seen my son look better, and I know it's all because of you. So don't thank me, it is I who thanks God for you. Steal all the attention and make them give you everything you want because you deserve it all."

He gives her another kiss to her forehead, turns and leaves, making his way out the doors and up the stairs to his room.

The moment he is gone Loralie bursts into tears. I wrap my arms around her as Adam, Zac and Lyncon give her a moment to take in the incredible man that is my dad.

We all took it upon ourselves to hide out here for a while. Between us all, we have tidied up the house and gardens, brought light in, and taken dirt and dust out, making it much easier to breathe.

The wood is chopped and stacked, and the kitchen is clean and freshly stocked with food.

While me and the boys have worked the house and gardens, Loralie has been keeping Dad distracted. We know he knows what we are doing but I think he's enjoying his time with Loralie.

I even think they have gotten so close that they are sharing secrets now from the way they clam up mid-sentence when we walk in. I don't mind at all, in fact, it fills me with great joy.

It's been five days since losing Trin. We are all doing our best, but we know the time is growing nearer where we must face what we have all been avoiding.

The funeral parlour has been trying to get in contact with Adam about the arrangements, but every time his phone goes off he shuts down.

He hasn't wanted to face their home without her any more than that woman wanted to face her sister's home without her ten-year-old niece.

Loralie takes the phone from Adam and gives him a smile. He doesn't take it back or stop what he knows she is going to do.

Over the next week Loralie busies herself making phone calls and setting everything up for the funeral until the day is finally here, the one we can't avoid, or at least that is what I thought.

Adam is gone when we wake. His bed doesn't even look like he slept in it. Dad is dressed in a handsome black suit and hot pink tie, a far sight better than his pyjamas, slippers and robe I have grown accustomed to over the last two years.

He has lost quite a lot of weight but thanks to Loralie taking in the suit, it doesn't show as much.

Loralie is wearing a hot pink dress and I am wearing a black suit and hot pink tie, the same as Lyncon, Zac and my dad.

As we were the closest to her we are all wearing her favourite colour in her honour.

The day is perfect and warm with a fresh light breeze. The black limo pulls up and the doors open.

The casket is a polished white, topped with an amazing bouquet of hot pink roses, tied with a thick, white, satin ribbon. Zac, Lyncon, Dad and I move to our sides, taking a silver handle each.

We move the casket out and we all seem to decide at the same time we are not taking her down that aisle on the silver trolly. We lift the casket up and on to our shoulders, sharing her weight amongst us. With every bit of pride, love and devotion we have for Trin, we begin to walk.

Loralie set it all up outdoors with loads of pink flowers and ribbons lining the aisle and pink petals on a carpet of white laid out with care on the green grass.

At the end is a beautiful white table and Adam dressed from head to toe in a suit of Trin's favourite colour, waiting at the end as I would imagine he would have done on their wedding day.

We all walk her to him as if we were all walking her down the aisle to give her away. We reach the end, place her down effortlessly, and give Adam our love on our way to our seats.

Through the whole ceremony Adam stood with Trin and when she was lifted and taken back down the aisle, Adam walked at her side, tears streaming down all our faces.

As for how she was to be buried, it was a closed casket. It was decided it would be sealed from the beginning so the last hands that touched her were ours.

At the end of the walkway was her final resting place at the top of a hill with the most beautiful view of the city under the shade of a beautiful willow tree.

Once she is in place, we all take a rope and lower her into the ground with perfect grace while Trin's favourite classical music plays.

Once everyone has said their goodbyes and dropped their roses on her casket, Zac, Lyncon and I all take off our jackets and ties and rest them on a nearby chair and grab a shovel each.

We all freeze when Adam stands over the hole containing the love of his life. He pulls the ring from his finger, tying it with a ribbon from one of the nearby flower wreaths to a single pink rose. He presses a long, soft kiss to its petals as his tears fall. He releases the flower, dropping it atop her casket, saying his final goodbye.

14

Chapter

Life has settled down a lot since Trin's funeral. Saying goodbye was harder than I had ever imagined. Since I never thought I had had much to lose, I never stopped to realise I have far more than I ever dreamed I would.

I get to wake up next to my wife most mornings and watch our miracle grow inside her. Loralie's belly is so big now it's hard to get close to Loralie without giving her a sneak attack from behind.

Time has flown by far too quickly and the time Loralie and I had at our cottage seems like nothing more than a memory. Victor has me so close to his side now I don't know where he ends and I begin. Before I was forced to be with Loralie all the time and now it seems they won't give me even a moment with her.

Dad seems to be doing much better. I think our company has brightened him quite a lot. Not that I'm around much. It's his time with Loralie I know he treasures. It does help a lot that they both love books and chess. Loralie even took Dad's place as undefeated champion.

Honestly, I thought Dad was bad enough, but Loralie is even worse. She doesn't even pretend you might have a chance.

Adam has not been back to his and Trinity's place. Me and the boys had to get everything sorted and sold the place, so he didn't have to worry about anything. I got everything put into storage like Lyncon suggested for when he is finally ready.

We tried distracting him with work, but things went horribly wrong when Adam got distracted and hesitated when he usually would have moved and in the end Zac got shot. Not badly, but still, it should never have happened in the first place, proving he's not going to be ready for a long time yet. So he just stays by dad's side and looks after him and Loralie.

Since I stood up to Bonney she hasn't interfered. That could also be due to the fact that I have been integrated into Victor's business now and Bonney has lost a lot of her power from the merge.

Zac and Lyncon are still in my mother's employ for the time being until Victor says he is satisfied with my work enough to let me choose my own men.

Victor seems happier now that I have become more compliant with his wishes under the promise Loralie is left with me.

I'm at a club of Victor's sorting out some issues when I get an urgent call to get to his house. The first thought I have is of Loralie, although I wasn't expecting her to drop the baby for another five weeks yet.

It doesn't take me long to get there but the moment I get to the gates I know something is seriously wrong.

They are torn down as if someone drove a truck through them, and once I get further up the driveway, I find the truck.

It doesn't take me long to realise the place is under attack. I back the car out and park down the road. I've already called Lyncon and Zac and they aren't that far away.

This could be my chance to show Victor how well we work together, and maybe I can choose my own team of men.

Zac is the first to arrive. I send Lyncon a message on where to meet us. We load up on guns and supplies and head around. I take the front while Zac takes the east entrance and Lyncon will take west from the other side. Lyncon messages he's in place and we move in.

Weaving through the front trees and bushes, careful to stay out of sight, I make my way up the stairs and into the house. Bodies of both Victor's crew and a group I have never seen before are strewn all over the front lawn and up the stairs. It looks like one hell of a battle was fought here.

In the main entrance is four more men dead and one hanging over the banister. I move towards Victor's studies where I have no doubt I'll find him. Seeing that the stairs are clear, I run up quietly, my gun ready.

I hear shots fire down the hall to the east notifying me Zac is in the house. I move in further, checking each room as I go until I get to Victor's door. Before I can open the door, it flings open. A large man is flung backwards past me as Victor barrels forward, emptying his barrel of bullets into the man.

"Hey Vic, I think he's dead," I comment.

"Not dead enough," He sneers, reloading and emptying another round into the man again.

"You are going to have to catch me up on what is going on at some point but right now I think everyone knows our position, so I suggest we move."

Victor reloads his gun again. "Let the fuckers come. I'll be ready."

He's barrelling past me before I know it. He is angrier than I have ever seen him before. I follow Victor as he charges down the hall without a care in the world, fury guiding him.

Bang!

Bang!

Bang!

Shots fire all over the place and bodies drop from all directions. A man leaps around a corner at Victor but before he has a chance, I fire my gun and the man drops.

Victor gives me a nod in thanks and moves on, quicker this time. It seems Victor is being a little more careful. Thank heavens, it's hard to protect a man with a death wish.

We move to a room somewhere in the middle of the house and come face to face with Lyncon.

"Shit man, I almost shot you," Lyncon says, a bit flustered.

"What does it look like down that end?" Victor asks, checking his gun.

"All clear."

"Good. Let's continue on. Stay sharp."

"Yes sir. Also, we should run into Zac so try not to shoot him," Lyncon winks.

Victor moves through the door and sure enough we find Zac in a tussle with another man. It looks like they both lost their guns and are now trying to kill each other with their bare hands.

"Hey man, you need a hand or you good?" Lyncon asks Zac casually.

Zac grunts while trying to push two huge hands from his neck. "I'm not too proud to say SHOOT THE FUCKER!"

Bang!

Lyncon fires his gun and the man drops on top of Zac.

"Come on man stop playing around. We got shit to do," Lyncon says, striding past Zac still pinned down by a man twice his size.

I shake my head with a smile, lean down and help Zac. Once he's free and back on his feet he gives me a look. "Why haven't we shot that dick yet?"

"You haven't shot this dick yet because you would miss me, and you know it," Lyncon's voice shouts through from the next room.

Zac and I look at each other and laugh as we join them. The whole house is cleared now and all backup has joined us, sweeping the area.

"What the hell was all that about?" I finally ask Victor.

He sighs, falling into an old-fashioned, red velvet chair by the fireplace. Lyncon and I do the same while Zac decides to remain standing.

"That was one of the groups we are partnered with, or at least we were. They burst through here saying we betrayed them, giving information about their organization. Stupid when you think about it. Why would we ruin a good friendship?"

"Looks like we might have a mole or maybe they do."

"Who would benefit from destroying our friendship with them and why? It doesn't make sense at all."

"Until we know more, we need to keep everything on lock down and start checking all the men."

Victor looks at Zac and Lyncon. "What about these two?"

"I have had them by my side for as long as I can remember. I trust them with my life." My response is clear, strong and confident.

Victor seems happy with it. "Very well. I think it's time you both came over to work with us. It will be easier to keep an eye on you both. I'll tell Bonney immediately. You all head off now and I'll see you all bright and early tomorrow."

Before I can answer my phone buzzes. "Dad, what's wrong?"

"It's Loralie. Come quick.

Before I have a chance, Victor is on his feet. "My car this way."

Without question, I move after him. Victor speeds to... my mother's home? What is Loralie doing here?

I open the door and bolt up the stairs and burst into the front doors.

I run down a corridor and I hear screams. Panicked, I run faster as a man bursts past me, knocking me out of the way. I let him pass and enter the room. Loralie is on the floor, blood staining the bottom half of her white dress.

15

Chapter

Loralie screams out, trying to get up but two men and three nurses hold her back.

"Alex, quick! Stop him! He's leaving with our baby!"

I turn and run out of the room, back after the man that knocked into me. I run without really knowing what is going on, when I bump into Victor. "What's wrong?"

"I have to chase a man down that just came through here," I say trying to push past, but Victor stops me.

"He's long gone now."

"What? And I should give up? Loralie just said he was leaving with our baby!" I snap, ignoring Victor and moving towards the front door.

With one click of Victor's fingers Lerch, Victor's right-hand man grabs me, stopping me from going after the man. I'm being turned around and shoved after Victor who is storming down the hall.

Victor turns when he gets to the room I left Loralie in and walks over to a hysterical Loralie and slaps her hard across the face. I see the look of hate and disgust on her face as she abruptly stops crying.

"Your behaviour is pathetic. You shame me," he seethes. I wiggle, trying to pull myself free as I watch Victor hit Loralie repeatedly.

"LEAVE HER!" My shouts are nothing to him as he continues.

"Why are you doing this? She is your daughter and she just had your grandchild. How can you treat her that way?" I yell my words as loud as I can and thank God he stops, turning on me.

"She did nothing more than she was supposed to do. Now it is done. Her behaviour is atrocious."

"I don't understand. That is my kid and I'll be damned if I let them leave."

"The child is already gone far from here as it was arranged from the beginning."

"What do you mean?"

"That was the deal."

I throw myself forward, pulling myself out of Lerch's grasp, forcing my foot back as hard as I can. I hear a crack and I know I have broken his leg. I run to Loralie, throwing them all off her.

I hold her in my arms, daring any of them to try me. "So then you have what you wanted from us. Now you leave us alone," I boom, forcing them all back with the fury in my voice alone.

Victor laughs, "Oh, no boy. The deal was that your mother raises the child and I... I get you."

My blood boils. "When will it be enough? When will you people stop taking from us? I am leaving with my wife, and you will not follow. You will leave us the fuck alone until we are ready to see you, or you give us back our child."

"I am sorry boy, but that child is already heading out of state as we speak. You will never see that child again, that was –."

"DON'T YOU DARE SAY THAT WAS THE DEAL AGAIN!" I yell, not even recognizing the mad man I have become. I am so filled with rage I can't even stand it anymore.

I am so angry I storm past all of them, Loralie still in her white, blood-stained dress. I cradle her protectively and leave quickly, not wanting them to think they can change their minds and come after us.

I know they will. Victor made it quite clear he saw me as his property and from the time I have spent with the man so far, I know what he is capable of. I know I will have a short while he will stay back, but if he has to come after me there will be hell to pay.

He doesn't give a shit if his daughter dies or if his grandchild is snatched away from his flesh and blood, but he cares if I return to his side? This does not sit right with me, and I am going to find out why.

I put Loralie in the passenger side of my Ferrari, not giving a shit if blood gets on the seat, and move quickly to the driver's side. Loralie is quiet. If it wasn't for the rise and fall of her chest I would question if she was alive.

I drive to Dad's, knowing I can't go far this time. I take her up the stairs to the master bedroom and place her onto the bed. She doesn't say anything. She just gathers her legs to her chest and looks out the window.

"I am going to go downstairs and get you something to eat or drink if you like," I say in hopes she will even give me a nod but I get nothing.

Every day is the same. I walk in with food and drink and leave with the last tray untouched.

I sigh. This can't go on much longer. She is going to die if I can't get her to eat something. On the tenth day I pick up the untouched tray and lose it. I throw the entire contents against the wall closest to her, smashing the bowl of soup and breaking the plate of toast and shattering the crystal glass of orange juice.

"Why are you doing this to me!" I yell, shaking the room with my anger.

"I lost our child too! Don't make it so that I lose you too." I drop sitting on the edge of the bed.

"You can't lose something you never had," her voice is barely a whisper.

"What?"

She doesn't repeat.

"What could you mean? We had a child, something that is yours and mine. I understand you lost your child but so did I. Don't shut me out too," I say, dropping my tone.

I feel the movement of the bed and before I realize it, Loralie is wrapping her pale arms around me, her mouth at my ear.

"Alex, you don't understand, and I hope you never do, but I am not in pain for me. I lost that long ago. My pain is for you."

I quickly grab her arm as I feel her try to retreat. "How can you be thinking of me right now when all I can think of is you?" I say, pressing a sweet kiss to her cold hand.

"I failed you."

"You didn't fail me. How could you even think that?"

She pulls herself free of me, refusing the comfort of my touch any longer. I reach, grabbing for her retreating arms.

"I don't deserve your pity! I don't deserve your love and I *don't* deserve your forgiveness. I am horrible and disgusting and I can't see why you still protect me," she cries, pulling from me like her touch will infect me somehow.

I don't understand what is going on and it looks like no matter what I say or do I am making things worse. I sigh and instead of leaving I take off my pants and shirt and climb into the bed.

"What are you doing?" she asks.

"I am sleeping. I am tired," I reply casually.

"That is not what I meant and you know it. Why are you not going back to your bed?"

"Because my bed is not as good as yours and I have given you too many nights alone. It doesn't seem to be helping you at all. So I give up. I sleep where you sleep," I say, pulling the blanket up around my shoulders.

"No, you need to leave. Did you even listen to a word I said? You need to go as far away from me as you can. Leave me!"

I simply reply, "No."

She huffs. Rather than argue with me anymore she pulls up a small blanket and huddles up on the windowsill.

I stay for a quiet moment listening to us breathe in and out. The sound is starting to annoy me. One more deep breath from Loralie and I'm out of the bed and scooping her up in my arms.

"Alex!" she shrieks.

"Say whatever you like you are my wife and I want you with me. If it was the fact I did something wrong and you couldn't stand to be near me, I could handle that but telling me your decision is for me, well I can't handle that. You said inside this marriage for all the things we have to deal with, we would accommodate each other's freedoms to make our own choices, so if your choice is you don't want me then I will respect that, but if your choice is for me, you have no right to take that choice from me when we swore we wouldn't."

My voice is rushed and breathless as I rant my frustration. Loralie doesn't seem to know what to say. I am right in all I said. I know she wants to be with me but thinks I shouldn't want to be with her. That is not her decision to make. It's mine.

I look into her green eyes and see her trying to raise an argument to fight me with but before she can voice it, my lips crash down on hers.

Loralie goes rigid for a moment but almost immediately relaxes, lost in the kiss just as much as I am.

I kiss her while I still cradle her in my arms. Loralie knows she has all the power to stop this for if I move my hands she will fall, but she doesn't. Her hands are gliding through my thick, brown hair, with one clench of her hands my head is pulled to her, deepening the kiss.

I walk to the bed trying to talk. "Lor..al..ie." She breaks for a moment, only a breath away. You aren't healed yet, nothing – ." Her mouth takes mine again, stopping my words.

Fuck, she isn't ready for sex yet. She can't be. It's only been ten days since she gave birth.

Her hands are ripping at my shirt, pulling it off my shoulders but it's trapped going any further because I'm still holding her. She pulls her feet from my grasp, planting them on the ground and forcing me to the bed. "Loralie, no. You need time."

Her hands are undoing my belt and pulling my pants from me before I know it. Fuck, I love how she takes what she wants.

"I've stopped bleeding and am more than fine. It's this, or we can go back to me running from you."

She smiles a wicked smile when I frown at her. She dives on top of me, kissing me once again. I give up trying to stop her, so I go with it, giving her whatever she needs from me.

Loralie's eyes light up when I raise my hands above my head, clasping them together, telling her without words I won't stop her from taking what she wants from me.

Her eyes brighten and change in a single moment from a childish girl to a sexy seductress ready to pounce. Her movements are slow and sensual. She glides her hands up her thighs, gliding the thin, satin fabric up her body and over her head. By the time it's off I'm so hard that I'm sweating.

She licks her lips as she moves off the bed to glide her knickers down her curvy thighs. I swear I'm drawling by the time they're off and she is crawling up the bed again. My hands are above my head. I still don't move. Her grin widens as she reaches my cock. Oh fuck! Her hot, rough tongue glides from base to tip in a slow tease.

She is testing how far she can go before I break and take control, but I won't. Not this time. Even if my dick bursts from the pressure I won't take this from her.

Her talented mouth tortures my cock to the point of madness but I don't break. Loralie's eyes meet mine and I see something shift in her, a vulnerability.

She climbs up, positioning me at her entrance and slowly sinks down my length. She lifts and drops her hips in a slow punishing rhythm, her eyes never leaving mine.

Her hands slowly cover over her body as if she just realized she was naked in front of me. My hands are down grabbing her hands gently removing them from hiding her breasts.

"Please don't hide from me."

She takes in a deep breath as if pushing herself to do as I ask. This girl is something new. She is shy and vulnerable. I've broken through.

I slowly place her hands on her breasts but this time I move her hands around her breasts. Then giving them a squeeze, she takes in a sharp breath as I pinch her thumb and finger over her right nipple.

"I thought you were not going to control this," she pants.

I smile wickedly, "You're doing it, not me."

Her fire renewed, she pushes my hands from hers, taking over completely once again. She raises herself, dropping on my cock with a force that shakes my balls.

Her pace quickens as she squeezes and rubs at her deliciously full breasts. I am beyond my bursting point, but I won't give in until she is ready for me.

She punishes my cock with every deep drive. The tight feeling of her soft, warm insides squeezing me tight.

She raises a breast to her mouth, drawing in a nipple, sucking it till she releases it with a little pop.

"Fuck, Loralie!" I grunt, trying desperately not to drive my hips up into her like I desperately need.

Her green eyes close as her head flies back, my name a cry from her lips. She comes long and hard, taking me with her. Loralie is still riding her orgasm as I empty myself in her.

I feel like a pile of goo by the time she flops on top of me. I laugh, "Glad to see I'm not the only one spent."

"Yeah, what's happening to us? Once we could go for days. Now we are exhausted after one," her laugh is pure and sated.

"I think it's quality, not quantity nowadays."

She smiles, "And what quality."

I can't help but smile back. She pulls herself from me and drops to my side and we fall asleep in each other's arms.

16

Chapter

I finally have a moment to look forward to today as I wait for the truck to pull around the turning space that now feels too small for this truck, but to my surprise, the driver does the job flawlessly.

I move to the back, practically bouncing out of my skin. The doors open and there he is.

Prince seems to be just as excited when he sees me. I race up the ramp the moment it hits the ground, not letting them unhitch him. I want to do that myself.

I open the gate and guide him out. The moment his feet touch the ground he spins around, obviously excited with the new place.

I laugh watching his excitement, trying to take in everything at once. "Easy Prince, we have plenty of time. This is your home now. Nothing but the best for you."

I begin to walk to the back of the property where Dad's stables are. The stocks are all full except for the one Dad said I could have for Prince once the old champion dash was retired and moved to the country estate.

I don't worry if he will run off. I know when he's had a run around he will find me. After everything he's been through I like to think one of us can have a bit of freedom.

Just as I reach the stables Prince finds me just as I thought he would. He acts more like a dog than a horse but I'm sure Dad will not be happy about a horse in the house so I stress to Prince he will have to stay with the rest of the horses.

I'm rubbing him down when I hear a scream coming from upstairs. I drop the cloth in the bucket and run.

I burst through the doors and up the stairs to find Lerch outside Loralie's room.

"For fuck's sake! Why can't you just leave us alone?"

"How dare you!" Victor's hand flies across Loralie's face so hard the impact knocks her to the ground. "Stupid bitch," he spits.

I struggle against Michael and Trevor who are a clear head taller than me, trying to get to Loralie. "Victor, Stop! She is your daughter!"

Victor turns his gaze to me, "I will get to you in due time boy." He turns his attention back to Loralie, smacking her to the ground again.

She doesn't cry or make a sound this time. Every time he hits her she gets back up. "Please stop it. Whatever you want, I'll do it. Just stop please," my voice comes out deep and strong, but I feel anything but when I see the blood on Loralie's face.

My words have Victor's attention, "Put her in the car and take her home. I have to teach Alex a few lessons."

Trevor releases me, grabbing Loralie and dragging her out the door to the limo. Trevor still holds me as Victor turns his attention to me.

"Do what you like Victor. As long as it isn't Loralie I'll be fine with whatever you give me."

"That's good news because I have much to give you but Loralie is stopping you from becoming what you are meant for."

I'm confused, is he going to hit me or not? Victor continues to circle me. "I have a vast empire with much to train you, and at this moment in time you being away while watching over a wife that is not doing what she is meant to."

"She is doing just fine. My wife is my business, no one else's."

"It becomes my business when you don't come to work or when issues arise and you are not up to scratch with what's going on. I know things have been rough but they are done. Get over them. A new day and the problem didn't go away. Boo hoo. Life goes on."

I feel my temper rising with every cold word he utters. "You lost your baby, get over it. We can beat your wife and take her away from you whenever we like. Get over it. We control you. It was the deal. Get over it!" I swear he says it one more time I'll....

"Until you can learn your place I'll have to take matters into my own hands, starting with Loralie. You seem to be most compliant when she is at risk. Hell if I know why. Do your job and get over I –."

Before he finishes the sentence I throw a massive punch, driving it into Victor's face so fast Trevor had no chance to stop it. Victor looks at me, rubbing his jaw.

"What? I hit you. Get over it." My words are ruthless and un-apologetic.

Victor breaks into a laugh, "Now that's what I was looking for. Give me that fire every day and everything will be yours. That's all I ask Alex."

"I want my wife in our home. You give me that with all the freedom to have a normal life with her outside of work and I'll do as you ask. You have my word."

Victor gives me a silent look as if thinking this over. "Very well, but you run off or try anything stupid and I will shut this all down again."

I hold my hand out to him and he takes it in his. "This does mean you won't hurt her anymore?" I say, pulling his hand closer, freezing our shake.

"That my boy is completely up to you," he says, pulling his hand back.

Victor pulls out his phone to call Trevor. The phone rings out. Victor's face becomes annoyed. "Ugh, good help is hard to find," he says, redialling the phone.

"Michael, let's go. We will probably get to the house before he even answers."

Victor, still on his phone, gestures for me to follow him. We walk out the doors and out to a waiting limo Michael has brought round for us. I get in right after Victor, not wanting to question anything, proving I will do as he asks.

Only halfway to Victor's we are stopped by flashing lights. Michael slows down. My stomach drops. Before anyone has a chance to stop me I am out of the car and running up the long line of traffic to where the police have the road blocked off and are redirecting traffic. Just beyond, I see the burning inferno that no more than an hour ago left my Dad's home with my wife inside.

I try to force my way across the barricade but am met by officers forcing me back and the more I push the more come.

"You can't go in there. It's not safe!"

"I don't care! My wife is in there!"

Six officers push me to a police car and throw me in the back, keeping me trapped as I watch the fire blaze fiercely. I don't know at what point the fire department gets here but the fire is so hot it takes a lifetime for the flames to die down.

I watch them guide cars around and push the traffic back further. Two ambulances are positioned to try and shield the incident while making sure they have clear access in case they find any survivors.

The fire is finally out and even though the wreckage has more water in and around it than most water parks, it still sizzles and steams.

The firemen finally move in, securing the sight. It doesn't take long before they are pulling a body out of the car and placing it on a white tarp.

My stomach drops and I feel my world come crashing down on me.

Only one body? Wait, there could be a chance that's not Loralie. My heart begins to race in hopes she managed to get out somehow.

That's when I see a pair of legs dangling from the back of the ambulance. I turn my head around further to see Trevor talking to two police officers while holding a shot up shoulder while a paramedic is dressing it.

Of course, Victor is through the barricade and at Trevor's side talking to the police as well. Once a few words are spoken to Victor he turns angrily to leave. His eyes dart to me and for a moment I swear I see... sorrow? Or maybe pity. Most likely for me.

My hope is gone. His look said it all. Even when his daughter is gone, taken from us, he doesn't feel for her even a little.

My hopes that Loralie is alive are dashed from me with that one look. Victor doesn't stay to make sure I'm okay or tell me the news himself. Well, I guess he just did with a single look.

If I could guess from the looks of Trevor and the vehicle, the car was attacked and after Trevor got out of the car to fight back, the car was set alight with Loralie still inside. With Trevor transporting her back to Victor's, the car would have been locked down to stop her getting out. Meaning once the vehicle was alight she was trapped. What better way to get at a king then to kill his one and only child? The only thing they never realized was that Victor holds no feeling for Loralie. His only weakness I can see now is me.

17

Chapter

I feel like a robot. I am at Victor's side day and night. Ever since the attack things have gotten crazy around here and Victor won't let me out of his sight. I work myself to exhaustion, effectively drowning out the world.

I could not stomach going to Loralie's funeral. I hid like a coward. I am a coward. Zac, Adam and Lyncon said it was a massive funeral, very beautiful, but I know there was no love in it.

Victor was mad as hell I didn't go but I know his whole lecture was only because I never gave him the chance to parade me as his poor widowed son-in-law.

I never realised how weak I was until I lost the only real thing I ever had. I work until I drop and unlike Adam and the aunty, I can't help but be in the room we slept together in. I return every day, tricking myself into believing she is still with me.

There's a wrap on my door at 5am and I answer already dressed. Sleep is not my friend nowadays. Michael stands ready to escort me like always. He doesn't tell me what is going on. He doesn't say a word. The moment he sees me ready he turn's and I follow.

It's been this way for a while. The haze that surrounds me is thick and unyielding, and ever since the attack there has been far more movement, with people coming in trying to knock Victor down.

We are at an apartment block that has just been vacated since Victor took it over, from the protesters outside to the angry evictees it has been hell securing the area for demolition.

The process is quite simple: implode the building into its own footprint. It is the general way to demolish massive buildings such as this and the safest.

One of the men from the blaster crew has come back to us to tell us that the detonations have been compromised again.

In times like these there is one man that jumps to mind to help the situation and I know it's going to bite me later. I'm dialling his number before I know it.

"Zac, somethings come up. I need your help."

"That's nice. I haven't heard from you since before Loralie's funeral."

"Look, I don't want any shit. Can you help or not?"

"For you to call me, it must be important so I won't tell you to go fuck yourself, but I will put a condition down that you at the very least give Adam a call. He's not doing well and you are his best friend or at least you're supposed to be. I know you have had a great loss but so has he. Get drunk together, get into a fight. I don't care, just do it together."

"He doesn't want to see me. You and I both know the one thing everyone is thinking but not saying is that Trinity's death is most likely my fault. If I didn't run off with Loralie she might still be alive."

"No one thinks that. You were gone for months and nothing happened."

"You really don't know how these people work and, in a way, I am grateful. I'll give everything I have to keep you as far from this as I can."

"We make our own choices Alex. If Adam wants to see you let him. He wants to punch you in the face... you decide if you let him. With us it's always been that way. We might not be able to control what goes on out there, but we can between the four of us."

"I won't make any promises, but I will think about it, and if you can't come out that's fine too."

I hear the phone go quiet for a moment, then, "I'll be there in twenty."

The line goes dead. That went easier than I thought, but I know he won't stop at that. Zac is well-known for his brains and determination as well as his insane intuition which I desperately need right now.

Just as he said he's here in twenty minutes with Adam at his side. Damn him, I knew it but still, he pisses me off sometimes.

They both walk up to me with perfect professionalism, "Report?"

I give Zac a nod and lead him over to the open tent that holds the architectural blueprints. While Zac is immersed in the plans Adam gives me a quick look that kills me.

He doesn't blame me for anything, but he's mad I haven't been there when he needs me, nor have I let him be there for me, making him feel worse or maybe he doesn't feel I think he's good enough to be there for me.

I feel a little knot in my chest and know if I let this go I'm going to feel more than I want. I am so not ready for that.

Zac starts talking, bringing me out of my thoughts. "Okay, first off I need a 3D printed version of the building and a 3D computer version. From the look of these notes, I think I'll have to take a look at the lower floors."

After checking these floor supports it will determine my suspicions but in the meantime besides the detonations, I think we might have to look at the fact someone is still inside, sabotaging them all.

I move out of the tent and start barking orders, "Do a thermal sweep and check all security. Also put security cameras up inside. Let's move."

After a few 3D computer models of the building have been demolished by Zac his suspicions were confirmed. If we proceeded with this demolition as it was, things would have gone wrong, causing more trouble for Victor and the family in the long run.

"Thank you for coming. I had a feeling something wasn't right. I didn't think it was with the demolition at all though. Your intuition is still as sharp as ever I see."

"Glad you still realise my worth to you."

I frown at him. "I have never underestimated your worth in any capacity, especially as a friend and most of all as one of four people I trust with my life."

"Your life but not your problems, right?"

"Come on Zac that's enough." Adam is standing in front of me, trying to shut Zac down.

"See Alex, he's just as hurt as you and yet he still protects you even from me. That is a real friend."

I hear what his tone is trying to imply. Hell, he's down right accusing me of being a shitty friend.

"You're right. I have not been there, mostly because I'm not here. At least I don't feel that I am. I sleep in Loralie and my bed as if she will be home any moment and work myself each and every day so that I am so tired it is only too easy to trick my exhausted brain the attack never happened, and if I see any of you, all you will do is force the fact she is gone on me, and like a selfish coward I would rather avoid the best friends I have ever known than except the fact my wife is dead."

Adam's eyes begin to water, and his arms are wrapped around me in a heartbeat. "I'm sorry."

"What the fuck are you sorry for?"

"I've been so angry, wrapped in my own way of grieving that I never thought your pattern would be different than mine."

"Everyone grieves differently."

"Yeah, but I wanted everything I love so close to me as if it would keep me from following after her, but you are the opposite, pushing everyone away, afraid to lose anything more and afraid to feel when it finally hits."

My chest burns from the pain struggling to be free and Adam is the one pushing it out. I hug him back, feeling the tears prickling at my eyes.

I hear one of the men come to the tent, releasing Adam quickly and composing myself as before, locking the demons behind a wall once again.

Just as Zac thought, the thermal imaging found two men hiding on the 10th floor in the air ducts. Between Adam and I running the new set up under Zac's directions we double check all the supports and change the locations on the lower floors just as Zac had thought.

With all new timing and the right explosives now in place and the two men in custody, we are all ready to watch the magic. There is something so satisfying about blowing up a building. With billowing dust clouds, the massive building implodes, dropping on the spot with perfection in a nice pile of rubble.

This technique needs so much skill. Not many would even attempt it let alone be successful in its delivery and even with knowing that I knew Zac would be flawless.

He's even that way in his personal life. Sometimes you have to get messy to root out the real problems. My fears and doubts in being a problem to my friend in pain are now gone, leaving me with nothing but my own self-pity and doubt.

The building has gone and the protesters have left defeated. Zac, Adam and I finish up with questioning the two men that were sabotaging the project.

Victor's men have been working them over for the last few hours but have not managed to get a thing out of either of them.

Zac walks in the room set up to hold them three blocks down from the demolition sight. The room is perfect, no windows and only one heavy door in and out.

One nod to the three guys working the two men and they all leave the room. One is white, blonde, tall and skinny, while the other is a head shorter with ash brown hair and quite stocky.

"You can do what you like. We ain't talkin.'" The stocky guy spits a mouthful of blood at Adam's feet.

Big mistake. Zac's face disappears behind his laptop screen and I move in closer, completely unfazed, while Adam steps back. It hurts because Adam would usually be in his element here.

After a quick look over the two men I see they have both had multiple blows to the face, ribs and hands, leaving them with broken noses, broken ribs and several broken fingers.

Torture of this kind won't work on men like this. This tells me these guys are from a rival organization, trained in this kind of thing. I pull up a chair between them and casually sit.

"Now let's talk. I know you are here to sabotage us and I know you're well trained. From the looks of how you break you know what broken ribs feel like, telling me you are not new to this ether. Everything you do tells us more than your words ever could so I don't need your words." The look on both of their faces drops for just a moment, showing a split moment of fear. "I am not as good with these needles as Adam is but I'll do my best not to let this go further than you can handle. I guess it's my luck there are two of you in case I mess up."

I am grinning inside when I turn and see a smirk on Adam's face when both men drop their fierce facades. Adam pulls out a small black zip up case just like I knew he would.

He unzips it slowly in front of both men, opening it for me to view the contents. I pull a small vial and a single long, thin needle. The blonde is the first.

"Please, we don't know much. We were told to be at that address and stop the demolition going right at any cost."

Zac pips in, "You're lying. You're Mark Boden and Jeremy Perkins. You both work for an underground organization that is being disassembled by Victor as we speak. That building we just demolished was once your bosses until it was seized in part payment of debt."

Both men go white. I grin widely, "See? I told you we don't need you to talk." I move in closer to the blonde Zac just identified as Jeremy Perkins. "Well Mr Perkins, this will hurt a lot."

I glide the needle slowly towards his strapped down hand as I torment him a little longer, that's when Adam places his hand on my shoulder.

I turn to him as he takes the needle from my hand and the small vial.

He's unscrewing the bottle and dipping the tip of the needle before I can protest. The look on his face is one I haven't seen in a while.

He's in work mode, clear and focused with no distractions. Zac is reading off more of their private information, from their kids and their schools to their in-home alarm passcodes, freaking both men out far beyond words before Adam comes in with his needles.

The men are shaken. "Please, we are only protecting our families. They're as good as dead if we fail and get discovered."

It pisses me off how easily he breaks under a little pressure. I know what protecting families is about, but men like him don't give a shit about family.

Zac is confirming that fact with a transfer into Perkins offshore account of ten million and the same for Boden, with open ended plane tickets out of the country not with or to their families.

One look at Adam and he has gloves on, slowly pushing the thin needle under Perkins's index fingernail. The scream that emanates from him is shrill and bone chilling, causing Boden to freak out, pulling and desperately yanking at his restraints. "Let me go and I'll do anything. I have no loyalties and neither does he. We have families in several countries. We could not care less. It's about the money and survival."

I'm surprised. I really thought Pekins would be the one to crack first.

"You know what we are capable of. In the last twenty minutes we have brought you to this point. Just think of what we can do as the time ticks on and we learn so much more."

"I know who you guys are. I've heard about you but the rumors were that there were four of you, not three of you."

"What? A guy can't have a day off? Tsk, tsk, tsk. There are four of us. I can make the call if you feel you need more company," Adam taunts, picking up his phone.

"NO!" both men scream.

Adam puts his phone back in the back pocket of his jeans, satisfied with the reaction he got. "Then tell us something Zac can't find."

"We know that no hit was put out for the fiancé and wife in your group and the incidents were set up from inside your organization."

"What?" I'm off the wall I'm leaning on. Boden has my complete attention. "Tell me everything you know."

"No one knows a lot. It was so well done there was not much left to investigate. No organizations have come forward and taken ownership of them. With such big hits to the Bright and Harlen families, you would think someone would. Serious activity was seen with Mrs. Bonney Harlen, then nothing. She vanished off the face of the earth and then there are the massive movements from accounts from within the Harlen family accounts."

"How do you know all this?" I ask.

"Just what I said. Guys boastin' 'bout what they found and how they got in. That's why when the two biggest hits came up everyone was wantin' ta know who dun it."

"What makes everyone think it was an inside job?"

"The word is a message was sent out from your very own Victor's home both times before each hit. If your man here can do all he dun with only a few minutes, he could prove I'm tellin' the truth."

I look to Zac and wait for him to give me something. When he finally does, my blood boils.

"It's true."

18

Chapter

Someone inside our organization is responsible. Adam and I look at each other. This means Trinity was no accident, and somehow I think we both knew it.

We release the men, knowing they would die if anyone found out what they told us, and at this rate someone else will get them soon enough, keeping our hands clean of the whole mess.

It's late so I take this chance to go back to my dad's place with Adam and Zac. They all seem shocked but I think I need a good stiff drink and some good company.

When we arrive Lyncon is waiting for us, sitting on the stairs. "Look what the cats dragged in. Finally miss us?"

"Something like that I guess."

"Well let's get you inside and glass in your hand." Lyncon pats me on the back, guiding me up through the massive heavy doors.

In the main greeting area is my dad. It breaks my heart to see him look so pale and fragile. His hands move in the air, one hand now holding a black polished walking stick.

He wraps his arms around me tighter than I thought he would be capable of. "Welcome home son."

I squeeze him back, happy to be home. I feel my phone vibrate in my pocket, disrupting our moment. "Sorry it's Victor."

I look at the message, *"was told things went well, why haven't you returned?"*

"Yep things went well. I'm here with my dad for the night. I'll be back in the morning."

"I don't think that is wise until we know who is behind all these attacks."

"Don't worry. I'm with the finest, see you at 5 tomorrow morning."

"If you insist. Stay safe and don't be late"

I spend the night drinking and catching up. Even Adam seemed to be enjoying himself too. Once things died down and the conversations became more serious Adam brought up the two men we came across today.

"What thoughts do you have on who's behind the leak?"

"Honestly I can see Victor organizing it but why get rid of your daughter and your son-in-law's friend's fiancée?" It makes no sense at all."

"It does if you want control."

"Wait, what are we talking about?" my dad asks, completely confused at the sudden turn to the conversation.

"Sorry Frank. We never mentioned the job we had today. Well the job Alex called us in to help with. In the end we found these two guys sabotaging the project and when we questioned them, we found out there was someone inside Victor's organization that set a hit on Loralie and Trinity."

"Wait, Trinity wasn't an accident?" Dad asks Zac.

"No, it's not looking that way at all, but I promise I am still looking into it all."

My dad looks devastated but not at all shocked about Loralie, but I guess we all knew the attack was fishy even for an attack.

Lyncon stands, his fists balled, "Excuse me. I need some air."

"Lyncon, I'm sorry we didn't mention this sooner. Are you ok?"

"Me? Two of my best friend's lost the women they love because of someone right under our noses and that doesn't make you sick to your stomach?"

"Of course it does, but you have to think who have we found in this miserable place that we could trust? Outside these walls there is no one else. So, honestly the list is huge and not one name out there will shock me, especially Victor's."

"It's no secret he didn't have high affection for his daughter but with her he had you. Doesn't your status as a widow mean you now have no part in his dealings without her?"

"No, I looked into that one. Since Alex was named, once Loralie married Alex he became adopted in the eyes of the law and without Victor removing it himself it will stay in place."

"When did that happen?" My question is more of a panicked blurt.

"The day you both got married it was in your marriage contract you signed, didn't you read it first?"

I have very little memory of that day. It all went by like white noise, I don't remember reading the contract which is not like me at all. From the look on my face, they are all thinking the same thing.

"I have never known you to put your pen to anything you haven't read thoroughly," Adam says in shock, looking at me like I grew another head.

"Yeah, okay. I fucked up. There is nothing much I can do about it now but it does make me want to find out why Victor has such a big interest in me."

It's 5am and I am feeling like utter shit. I was up all night talking things over with Zac, Dad, Lyncon and Adam.

"Right on time but you look like shit." Victor is ruthless with his observations. "I guess this works out well. Michael will take you home. Get some sleep and be ready by midnight tonight. I'm taking you underground."

I don't argue I just do exactly as I'm told. I get back to the hideously huge place Victor gave Loralie and I, now it's only me It seems even more stupid, but Victor won't let me stay away from here because apparently it sets a standard for the family's power and strength.

Apparently, I need one-hundred-fifty bedrooms, sixty offices, forty-eight bathrooms, twelve kitchens, and twenty-four lounge rooms not including the nineteen major bedrooms that are full suites, which I have been staying in the grandest of all.

I sigh. I hate this place. At no point did this place ever really show Loralie was ever here except her clothes that they cleaned out the day she died. Dad's house is the only place that has anything left of her now.

I walk up the stairs and down the long hall until I find my room. Although I guess it wouldn't matter what room I was in. Some of the other rooms must have staff in them, I just never see any.

I open the door and walk inside, throwing off my clothes as I walk to the massive bed. The large blackout curtains are drawn, darkening the room enough to trick the body it's night time.

I lift the covers and jump into bed. It doesn't take long before I feel the sweet pull of sleep. A movement beside me jolts my sleep away again. I'm about to grab my gun when I get a whiff of mixed perfumes.

The moment my brain registers the smell several arms wrap around me. I quickly pull free, launching to the light and flicking it on. The sudden invasion of light is blinding but soon illuminates five very beautiful young naked women in my bed.

They all sit on their knees coaxing me to join them in the bed. That's when I notice the sashes each of them is wearing. Fuck, they are all beauty queens.

It's at this very moment I know I am fucked. Five of the most beautiful women in the world. It has been so long my balls are so big it hurts when I walk.

I know Victor is trying to shower me with beautiful women to help with that problem but they aren't Loralie and no matter how desperate I am, none of these women even make my dick twitch.

They are all disappointed when I thank them politely and usher them out of my room so I can get some sleep.

By twelve o'clock I'm up, showered and ready for whatever Victor has for me tonight.

"Okay boy, we have lots to show you. Things are getting messy and time is getting shorter. I'll be taking you around a few of our main sights. While I'm taking care of some business, I'll be trusting you to keep an eye on things and make sure everything keeps running smoothly in my absence."

I nod so he can continue telling me about what is expected of me while he is away. After all this time I know how Victor works now. He does not like you speaking at all unless he asks you a direct question that needs more than a nod or shake of the head.

Victor is finally taking me to one of the black spots we have in the organization. I know there are things that are not right here but I am the spawn of evil and there is nothing I haven't seen or that would shock me anymore.

Well, that was what I thought and how wrong was I. Victor takes me to a shipping container yard off the docks.

We go through a few rows until Victor stops and opens one that is empty, but he still walks in. At the back of the container, he pulls a lever you would think would open the door on the other side that is pressed hard up against another container, but instead, the floor shifts, revealing a staircase. He goes down and I follow behind him. After a while the stairs stop at a door. Victor puts in a code and another door opens, revealing a mass of underground tunnels and large rooms.

One by one we pass dozens of rooms and every one of them has a different horror inside. It takes everything I have to keep my face neutral, showing this doesn't bother me at all.

"These rooms are for the rich and wealthy people who pay us to live out their wildest fantasies no matter what they are." I go past a door where a man is fucking a woman as he shoves one of her body parts into a tank with what I assume are piranha.

"We don't say anything if the price is right. We give them what they want and the privacy to do it in. The sicker the demand the higher the price."

"Somehow I think this is horror movie shit we are talking about."

"Oh, no son. This is way worse. There is no hero and every scream is ignored. This is hell and we rule it all."

We keep walking and I glimpse in each window and sometimes I see something I wish I didn't, but I keep looking anyway. Fuck. Am I sick?

No, I am taking in everything and anything so someday maybe I can get out of this hell. No, that will never happen for me. This is hell, and I am being pulled deeper and deeper every day.

Victor keeps walking down the tunnel when a door flies open to my right and a beautiful young woman with African features falls half naked in front of me. She looks up and grabs at my leg.

"Please help me!" she screams. Around eight short, fat, balding, old men are at the door all in different stages of undress.

Casually they lean in the doorway when they see Victor. "Ah, it seems you have found our toy," one of the men chuckles.

"Yes, it looks like we have. You should be more careful not to lose it in a place like this," Victor smiles back.

The men move toward the girl. Arms reach for her as she kicks and screams, still clinging to my leg. "No! Please, you can't let them take me! Please!"

I bend down to her as cold as ice and go straight to hell with what I say next. "We are not heroes. We are not here to save you. With the right price you can do what you like and we won't judge. Scream all you like. No one will come and no one will care. Welcome to hell."

I forcefully grab her by the hair and pull her from my leg, throwing her to the wolves. She is not even back in the room before she is naked and being fucked in every orifice you could fit your dick into. I turn from her, begging the demon inside me to take over and stop this gut-wrenching sickness I feel eating me alive.

Victor seems to glow as he reaches the end, putting in another code into the next door and it opens to the same sort of thing, tunnels and rooms all the way down. This stretch is less messy. There is less blood but it is just as bad. Men are throwing unwilling women into rooms by any means necessary, by their hair, arms, dragging by their legs, you name it.

Although people are not being dismembered and tortured in this space something just as evil is going on here.

Cries and whimpers fill the stretch as we walk. "This area is not as high end as the higher section. This is reserved for the black-market sales and prostitution."

"These women do not look like they are willingly here," I scoff, playing my part so well I scare myself.

Victor grins at me widely like a boy showing his best friend all of his most treasured toys. Every gleaming tooth he shows me I want to punch out.

"We have women from all over the world brought here. No woman here was taken from American soil. No one would think of looking for any of them here and by the time they have fulfilled their usefulness they are sent to the fantasy tank and then thrown in the incinerator.

Is it just women we deal with?" I ask in my most interested tone I can muster.

"Heavens no, our demands are just not that high for men or boys so they are sought on demand, but if you come this way, I will show your gift."

"Gift? I thought this was about business."

"Oh, my boy, there is always time for a good gift amongst work. Makes things more fun don't you think?"

I give him an agreeing smile while my stomach turns at the thought of what it could be, especially housed in such a place.

He opens a far door and I follow. Inside are women that are cleaner and prettier. *Oh, fuck no.*

"Since Loralie is gone now you need to think of the family and your responsibilities. Choose one of these women and I will adopt her into my household. You can marry her. They are all fine, well-trained women. Watch."

He raises his hand and they all stand quickly, quietly and gracefully. He walks over to one, striking her hard across the face. She drops to the floor, and it takes everything I have not to move to help her up. She recovers quickly without a sound and is back on her feet standing as if nothing had happened to her, just like I had seen Loralie do.

He moves behind a red head and rips the thin fabric dress from her body exposing her to me completely. She doesn't flinch.

Victor moves through the rows of women, stripping them, striking them, testing them and each and everyone plays her part perfectly.

This all seems too familiar to me and that is when it hits me. The realization hits so hard I have no time before I am ejecting the contents of my stomach.

Fuck I can't show him weakness! I can't show him weakness! I can't! FUCK!

19

Chapter

I lose it. I am on Victor so fast he doesn't have a chance to stop me. "You put your own daughter through this?" I look into his eyes and feel even more sick. "Loralie is not even your daughter is she? Loralie was one of these women, wasn't she?" I demand, forcing his back against the far wall as hard as I can.

It doesn't take long before his dogs come running in to stop me from fucking up their boss. He instantly waves his hand and everyone leaves.

Victor looks at me without any fear and rests his hands on mine. "Let me down, son, and I will tell you everything you need to know."

"Bullshit! You would not know the truth if it introduced itself to you," I hiss.

Again, Victor pats my hands. "Come son, I am getting old, and time is short. No more secrets. Let me down and I will tell you everything."

I look into his eyes and choose to believe him. If I am going to get any answers this has to be on his terms, I know that, so I let go and take a step back from him.

Victor walks around me like a vulture would circle its prey. But I follow his every move around me.

"Yes, Loralie was from here. She was trained to be everything the organization needed your wife to be. Her real name is Willow dee Vance.

"My high school girlfriend that went missing?" I couldn't know they were the same girl. She has grown up so much since then but once I showed I cared for any girl she went missing so I stopped trying. Now I find out they all had a fate worse than death because I dared to care about them.

FUCK!

"Are you telling me every girl I ever liked is here?"

"Not all but the ones with merit. They were brought here but not many passed. Most ended up in the fantasy room then the incinerator. Loralie was the only original of your choices that made it through."

I feel the bile rising and it takes everything I have to stop it from coming up.

"What is the training?" I ask, not wanting to know yet needing to know what Loralie ... I mean Willow went through to end up with me.

Victor looks at me for a moment then walks me out of the room. Once he's out he opens the door to a room to his right.

Inside are women fresh and young, some no older than twelve. "These women have been selected for training. They will be beaten and raped until they stop fighting and stop screaming. Once they are broken, they are trained. If they fail, they are taken to the fantasy section where people pay a massive price for one final play. From there you know the rest, but if they succeed, they are adopted into high end families and married off to produce children.

Every woman in here is fucked with no protection. Every child born from these women are taken from them at the moment it is born, and she is fucked until she falls pregnant again. Every baby born here is sold on the black market for incredible prices because of our large turn out and high end variety."

Willow, my poor Willow. What did they do to you? She was forced to give up child after child. She was prepared to give up our baby, but it was me, she said it herself, it wasn't her pain she was worried about it was mine. She called herself disgusting and said she didn't deserve my pity or protection. This explains *so* much.

Victor clears his throat, preparing me that there is obviously more. Fuck, I don't think I can handle much more right now.

"Why would you do all this? She wasn't even your daughter. *Why?*"

He sighs. "You're right she isn't my daughter. I was only ever able to father one child, a son. I played with my best friend's wife, and she bore my son, and to save us the scandal and us both losing more than the scandal was worth we devised a plan."

I look at Victor in horror. "Your... best... friend?" I stammer.

"Frank is not your biological father Alex, I am."

I blink a few times, not registering what he is saying to me.

"Your father could not produce an heir. Your mother and I met at a party, and we couldn't keep our hands off each other, and wouldn't you know it, she fell pregnant with you. We agreed you would be raised as their son and when you were older you would take over my company through marriage to make it legal and your mother's miss deeds would never come to light and my son could legally take all I have without suspicion or scandal."

I can't breathe. The only thing I ever cared about that I thought they could never take from me was my father and his love, and in one sentence it's gone just like that. The only man that truly loved me is not my real father and not only that, but my slut of a mother betrayed him with his best friend.

FUCK!

Victor doesn't say anything more. He waits for me to adjust, but there is no way I'll be adjusting to this any time soon. "I'm sorry. I can't do this, I'm out."

"Son please listen to me."

"NO! Don't call me son! I am done listening. This is way too much. You betrayed your best friend, you lied to me, and now you think you can step in and take the one thing I have left? You will never be my father. I have one, the greatest man I have ever known and you are not him. How dare you stand there and rip apart everything I ever cared about."

I'm pacing as I throw my hands in my hair, not really knowing what to say or do. I stop and think for a moment and everything becomes clear.

"This is why you never really showed any care for Loralie... I mean Willow, and it's also why you had such a strong interest in me. This is also the reason you and my dad drifted apart." My voice is soft and low as I run through everything that now screams his telling the truth. I can't handle this anymore. I turn for Victor and begin to walk.

"Alex, you will come to see things my way and realise everything was for the best. I know I wasn't there for you but if people found out I had a real son you would be the biggest target the world would ever see."

His words don't stop me. I walk out. I don't say anything, I just walk. No one stops me. I walk past the women being raped. I walk past the beatings. I walk past the babies crying as they are ripped from their mothers. I walk past the incinerator room that I know runs all the time. I walk past the room with the pale corpse of the woman that once screamed for my help that now lies naked and dead on the floor.

I walk past the next room with a torso with no arms, legs or face anymore, no doubt the remains of the piranha victim. I walk up the stairs and out of hell desperate to breathe fresh air.

I breach the surface and exit the shipping container. I walk to the main road that was much further than I originally thought, one of the main reasons it's so well hidden, I guess.

I raise my hand and finally flag down a taxi on the opposite side of the road. While we drive, I try to process everything but don't get far.

It isn't long before I find myself right in front of my dad's family home. The driver pulls up and lets me out after the best tip of his life. I know why I came here. I need to see my dad.

My feet take me through the house right to where I knew I would find him, sitting in his favourite chair reading a book in the massive library he loves so much.

I stand in the doorway for a moment watching him in his element reading a book. I recognize the one he's reading as one of the best sellers Willow had given him, Brotherhood and Betrayal by E.G Never.

I find myself lost in how appropriate the title is at this moment in time.

Dad notices me and immediately marks his page with the bookmark I made for him when I was five. He removes his reading glasses, placing them together on his side table, giving me all his attention just like he always does.

I can't help it. My eyes tear up and my heart breaks. This man is in every way my father and I don't give a fuck what they say. I have one selfish part of my life I am keeping and there is no way I am giving him up.

He smiles, not a single hint of judgment on his face as he opens his arms, inviting me in to embrace him, so I do. I get down onto my knees and hug my father, the man who raised me, the man who protected what he could of my soul, the man who showed me love.

"He has been desperate to tell you for so long. I always knew this day would come."

My eyes fly open and I pull away only enough to see his face.

My father only looks at me with love, "You know?" I ask in disbelief.

"I knew your mother was having an affair and I knew Victor was the one that gave you the life I failed to give you, but that means nothing to me. You are every bit my son and I love you."

His words cut me deep and I can't help but let the tears fall. He is the only man I show weakness to. He thumbs my tears as they fall, never judging me for a second.

"How did you ever forgive her?" I ask.

"How could I not? If she never did, I would not have had the pleasure of having you as a son. You are the brightest thing that has ever graced my life and that has given me more joy and fulfillment than any amount of money or power. Victor didn't get that, I did."

"You and Mum never really acted like you were in love, is that why?"

"After she had you things were never the same between Bonney and I. She was making plans for your wedding day long before you were even born and no matter who was suggested outside of Victor, she found every reason to push the possibility out only leaving Victor's family. That's when I decided to look into things. I knew the likelihood of having kids was only a miracle. I was so angry and hurt because of her betrayal and the fact you were not mine. I stood by her side when she delivered you and I had no intention to ever look in on you again after that moment but when the nurse shoved you in my arms, I was captivated completely. I didn't care what came my way. I would face it knowing I was a father and you were mine. I held you first and I swore I would love you long after my last breath was drawn."

His smile in this moment fills me with hope and love, melting my frozen heart for one split second. Then I hear it whiz past my face. I feel the slight graze across my cheek.

His eyes are still on mine, his loving smile never leaving me. The bullet hits him in between the eyes.

I wrap my arms around his body as it falls back in his chair. I am so confused. It all happened so fast and yet in slow motion. The ringing in my ears is still sending my senses into chaos.

I look around, trying to find something that makes sense. And that's when I see her, my mother standing at the doorway with a fucking gun in her hands.

I pull his body closer to me. "Why!" I growl through my teeth.

"Because he made you weak," her every word dripping in disgust.

20

Chapter

I am too shocked to move or register what has happened. I cradle my father's lifeless body as the sound of Bonney's high heels clop loudly on the polished marble floors.

"Why?" I hiss. The words come again, finally finding a small part of my brain.

"I told you why. Once Victor told me he was telling you I came as fast as I could, but he had already done it against my wishes, and knowing you would run to Daddy I came straight here to do damage control."

Her words are careless as she removes her white travel gloves now obviously covered in gun residue.

"He always knew. You didn't need to kill him. He always knew!"

She looks down at my dad's body still in my arms without a care or a hint of remorse. "Oh well. It was his time anyway. Parkinson's was not killing him fast enough."

I let my dad's body down, sitting him gently in his chair and I rise to my feet. Bonney stairs me down without fear.

"Victor gave you a selection for a new bride. Pick one and get things back on track. We need an heir and you need to fix things with Victor since you walked out on him. He's worried and thinks you're unstable right now."

I listen to her dribble as my pain rolls into rage, bubbling beyond anything I have ever known.

"Why do I need to give you another heir when you already have one?"

"Everything has been taken. I came back to get Victor's help. Everything we had is gone, seized. Without Victor we are sunk, so you will get your ass back to Victor and tell him you agree to everything he wants."

My hands are shaking with rage. I can't think of anything greater than killing my mother in the most horrific way.

She strides past me. "Get this mess cleaned up. At the funeral we will say he finally succumbed to his sickness."

"Don't you think the bullet hole in his head will be a dead giveaway?" I spit in fury.

"They will say what I want them to say with a closed casket and no one will know none the wiser."

"Where is my child?" I hiss as calmly as I can.

"David is none of your concern. We have far more important things to worry about."

"David? I have a son?" I ask a little more pleasantly with this new information.

She looks at me realizing what she just did. She thinks for a moment. "Yes, I named him David Alexander Harlen."

I have a son. It doesn't matter what I lose. I still have more that they can take from me and even control me with. I release my fists knowing I can't hurt her if I want my son's safety, the only thing I have left of Loralie.

Just as Bonney said, Dad's death was written off as his Parkinson's finally taking him.

I watch on as the only parent that ever loved me is sent off in the most public show. It makes me sick. I look over to where I see my mother dressed in black. Her performance is award winning. She is crying real tears, real fucking tears!

I grit my teeth thinking of all the ways I wish I could watch her die. A bullet to the head is far too quick for her. I hope when her time is up I am there and I hope it is good because if I can find a way, I will sell my soul to the devil for the chance. I want her out of my life for good.

The altar has a big, flashy casket, closed of course. His body is already cremated. This is all for show and the demon bitch in the front is putting on a great one.

A hand reaches out in front of me. The clink of ice against glass and the sweet smell of bourbon brings my attention to Lyncon who is at my side holding out a glass to me. I take it and he clinks his against mine.

"To the old man," he says, holding it up to the roof then downing it in one gulp. He looks at me as if pushing me to do the same because he is ready for another one. I down the glass just the same and Lyncon takes it before I finish lowering it.

I look on after him. One of my best friends is obviously hurting just the same as I am. I have been so lost in my misery and hate for the she-devil, I didn't think of what this was doing to anyone else, least of all those closest to me.

Zac comes over, following Lyncon who has returned with another bourbon in hand for each of us.

Zac looks at the floor, not knowing what to say. Lyncons mouth twitches.

"Someone say something!"

Zac jumps slightly. "Come on, man. What is there to say?"

How is the weather? The bourbon tastes like shit. This is a fucking sideshow. Any of these help the situation?" I say dryly, emptying the amber liquid in my glass again.

Zac opens his mouth to say something but chooses against it.

"When you have fun, we have fun. When you are pissed, we are pissed and if you lose something we lose something. That is just how we work. It has always been that way man." Lyncon takes my glass from me again the moment he finishes his own, just as before.

Zac looks after Lyncon, then at me, "Frank was a father to all of us. We have been together so long you can't blame us for feeling shitty too."

"I don't blame any of you for anything. I just hate being here amongst all of this shit," I say, shoving my hands deep in my pockets, not liking them on the loose.

"Then let's go get the fuck out of here," Zac says, a little hopeful, the tension obviously getting to him.

"Adam! Let's go!"

We are all back at Dad's and drunk in no time, sitting around our normal lounge room Dad had set up only for the five of us.

The night is full of memories we all have of different moments with Dad, remembering him in every detail. Since I managed to get Dad's ashes, we placed his irne in his normal chair while in this room.

"I just found out I have a son." The room goes silent. "Yeah, David Alexander Harlen."

All eyes are on me. "She actually told you?" Adam sounds shocked.

"Yeah, I think she accidently did it because it took her a moment after she realized what she said."

Lyncon looks at me with a grim expression on his face.

"What's with the face?"

Lyncon looks at Zac who does not look comfortable at all.

"What's going on? Tell me!"

"We kinda went looking for information on why Bonney came back and what we found was pretty bad." Zac looks at Lyncon again as if asking him if this is a good idea to tell me.

"Tell me damn it!"

Zac sighs. "Someone has been feeding information to the police, slowly chopping off all the little parts of the organization. Everything Bonney and Frank owned is now gone or at least they are in the process of being taken."

"She did mention something about that before, but I thought she was exaggerating."

"No, not at all. In fact it gets worse. Bonney is testifying that all of the illegal activity was under the commands of Frank. She pinned everything on your father and since he's dead he can't testify his perky bimbo wife was the mastermind."

My stomach turns. She killed him to save her own ass. It was never about me.

Zac, Lyncon and Adam are all quietly looking at each other not knowing what to say. There is nothing you can say to a brother that has lost his wife and father all in a small space of time and I am done losing anything more. I jump to my feet and make a phone call.

I up and left Adam and the others to drink but I know they are worried about me and they should be. Right now I'm being driven by rage, the copious amounts of alcohol useless to drown out the pain that is wreaking havoc on me right now.

I'm let out of the SUV Victor sent me and make my way to the shipping yard. I go through the towering containers until I find the one Victor took me to last time.

I open it up, move to the back and pull the lever. Once I get to the door with the security panel Victor is already there with the door open.

Victor smiles triumphantly, holding his arms out to me to embrace him, without hesitation I do. He pats me on the back, guiding me through the tunnels to the rooms. Once through the fantasy section that is quiet and uneventful, I'm out the back in an office Victor has set up while he's down here.

"Okay my boy, I'll have a few documents for you to sign after we discuss all the finer details, and we still have the matter of the bride."

"Choose whatever one you like best. Honestly I could never decide. I'll do my part and in return you know what I want. Has it been arranged?"

"What you asked of me is no easy request but thanks to recent issues it has made your request far easier. Sign that contract and I'll make sure your wish is granted this very night."

My eyes widen a little in interest, "So soon?"

"My son asks something of me for the first time, I'm sure as hell going to give it all I have."

"You will have no issues with this request?"

"Not at all," he grins widely.

I sign the paperwork without reading it. I know my fate is sealed and with this request. The expectations of me will be worse than ever and I know without a doubt I just sold my soul to the devil.

Victor stands and waits at the door for me to follow so I do. Once out the door he moves through the tunnels to the fantasy rooms.

As we walk I see that all of the rooms are empty for a change. I can't believe how relieved I am not to see any innocent women suffering here tonight. Halfway up Victor turns into one of the fantasy rooms.

It's huge, at least twice the size of any of the others. I look around the room. The walls are a soft cream, and the lighting is quite bright. In the middle of the room is a massive bed with white satin sheets.

Everything in this room is white, from the racks full of straps, belts, ropes and ivory handled knives to the bed table and chairs.

The ceiling has harnesses, straps and chains hanging from it and over to the far side is a bubbling white bathtub.

I stand in the middle of the room with the greatest feeling I've had in a long time, a feeling that reminds me that I am a sick and twisted man that is about to unwrap the best present a disturbed boy's Daddy could ever give him.

The door opens as Bonney is thrown inside. She falls to the floor in a heap, blindfolded with her arms tied behind her back.

"Let me go! Victor won't stand for this! Do you know who I am? When I get out of here I'll have all your heads!" she yells, her voice bouncing off the walls as she spouts her abuse without a single fear.

I stand behind Bonney as Victor moves in front of her. Slowly, he removes her blindfold.

"Victor?" she gasps and pulls at her bindings while trying to regain her composure. "What is all this about? Baby you know if you wanted to play this game all you had to do was ask," she chirps seductively.

"This isn't a game. This will be the last place you ever see." Victor says the words with no feeling at all, causing Bonney to show signs of fear.

"Haha! You're joking, right? You wouldn't do that to me. I am the one that has given you everything you ever dreamed of. I have thrown my husband's organization into ruin, giving it to you. Every major client you have ever gotten came through me," Bonney says though her teeth as she struggles against her bindings.

"You think Alex will do anything for you if you so much as breath on me wrong? I suggest you let me go and we just pretend this little misunderstanding never happened."

Victor grins widely, bearing every one of his perfect teeth. "Oh, Bonney darling, it is not my wish you are here, but I am enjoying this more and more, I must confess."

"If not you then who would you do something like this for?" her words lash out angrily.

"Me," I say, stepping round so she can see me. As I slowly walk around her, my mother's eyes follow me with her mouth agape. "Hello mother."

21

Chapter

"This is your doing? You wouldn't dare hurt me. I will make sure you never see your child if you do." She tries to gain composure, but ends up stuttering her words. Her eyes are slits. "You think you can treat me this way?"

"Are you forgetting the situation you're in? We are deep underground. There are no heroes here and no one will come to save you." I see Victor smirk at my choice of words he's heard me use down here before. "And you have gone so far that not a soul will care when you're gone."

She looks to Victor with a seductive pout, "That's not true, is it Victor?"

He kneels down to be face to face with Bonney. "I didn't do this to you Bonney, you did. You let all of your men down, you let danger leak into my family compromising my organization, not to mention you failed my grandchild and most of all my son."

"*My son!*" she hisses, spitting in his face.

Victor pulls out a hanky from his pocket and wipes his face calmly, then looks at me. "May I?" he asks me.

"Be my guest," I grin.

The moment I say the words Victor flings the back of his hand across Bonny's face. She falls to the side, her head hitting the ground with a hard thud.

Slowly, she pulls herself up using her forehead as her hands are still tied behind her back. Once she is upright, Victor swings, knocking her down again. This time when she comes up there is clear swelling and redness to her cheek and blood at the corner of her mouth. "Kill me if that's your wish."

"Oh, not mine Bonney dear, your son's. As you can see, his wishes are gladly mine to grant."

Victor stands and walks over to the door as I move into Victor's spot. "Oh, you will die but not before you suffer long and hard for all you have done. Tonight all of your fears will be brought to life. Oh, and you, my beloved mother, are one such wish Dad has gifted me." I live in that moment when the word 'dad' rolls off my tongue for Victor in far more affection than her name ever has, and in her knowing this arrangement is both Victor and my doing.

I stand as Victor wraps on the door and two men walk in, one a tall, skinny man named Doug with ginger hair that looks like his mental status is hanging by a thread, and the other is a very tall, beefy, African man named Theo. I delight at the look on her face.

She has a massive fear of Asian, black and ginger men being near her, let alone touching her. She is probably the most racist person I have ever met.

Theo walks over to her and scoops her up like she weighs nothing. Bonney struggles and screams, "Don't you touch me you filthy disgusting thing!" Theo doesn't react. He effortlessly removes the ropes from her hands, moving to grab for the leather bindings hanging from the ceiling.

"Not those ones," I say, nodding my head over to the chains. He nods and does as I ask. I don't want her to be comfortable in any way.

With Bonney screaming and flailing, each of her hands and feet are fastened into each cuff that is locked with a key at each point. She now cannot move her arms down or put her legs together.

I lean against the white table and watch as Doug excitedly pulls out a small pouch of needles and a small vial. He dips each needle into the vial as Theo holds her feet in place.

Bonney screams with each needle that is inserted under each of her perfectly manicured toenails. When every toe has settled from the long, fiery pain the little vile provides and each toe has darkened from the build-up of blood, Theo stomps his large foot on each of hers.

Bonney howls a scream when Theo lifts his foot each time. At least three nails from each foot come off at the same time, oozing blood all over the white floor.

"Where is my child?"

"Please just kill me! I can't take any more!" she cries.

"Oh no, we have only just begun," I smile. I move to the door not wanting to see this part. Once I'm at the door I open it to find five more men in the doorway, a Scottish man with ginger hair and another man darker than I have ever seen, one Chinese man, and one Filipino man and one very excited looking Mr. Tanaka.

Since he was the one person she has hurt the most, I thought he deserved the right to take his own revenge, and he didn't turn down the opportunity.

One look at Tanaka and Bonney gasps and pulls at the chains binding her. "No, get away! Don't touch me!"

The door closes behind me and all I can hear are her screams. Right now she will be fucked by all of those men until they are satisfied and only after that will they cover her enough for me to enter.

I may be fucked up, but no kid ever wants to see their parents nude or having sex. I'm on my fifth cup of coffee before each of the men begin to leave the room one by one.

The last is Tanaka. He gives me a bow as he leaves with the most content look on his face. I know that was a dream come true for him. As much as he was victimised by her he was still very attracted to her.

I enter the room again once I get the all clear she is covered. When I see her, she is hanging, her legs unable to hold her weight, the shackles at her wrist's cutting into her causing her wrists to bleed.

She is well and truly bruised from strong forceful hands and her face, mouth and body are covered in semen. The only thing covering her is a thin piece of white sheet that is tied diagonally across to her left shoulder with a pin holding it closed at the same hip, easy enough to expose her again but enough to keep my stomach contents in place.

"No more. Please," she begs weakly.

"Already? That was only round one. The next batch of men will be here right after your next makeover."

"No, please!" she cries.

I pull up a chair as Doug moves to a scalpel set. He opens it and sets it up on a small table to his left. Once he has everything set up, Theo holds Bonney firmly from behind, removing the top half of the thin piece of material left to cover her body, exposing her breasts.

I shift a little not being entirely comfortable with this part but once Bonney's face changes the moment she sees the blade at her breast I forget everything.

Doug gives her an injection to slow the blood then cuts the tissue perfectly under her breast just enough for the breast implant to be removed. Bonney's screams and cries are magic as each one hits the ground with a plop.

"Where is my child?" I repeat again.

"Just kill me" she heaves.

I sigh and leave the room again as Doug sews her up and the next round of men enter. Her cries ring out loudly, her fear renewed.

I move down the hall to the area Loralie knew only too well. The entire place is quiet, obviously shut down for the night for my request.

I open a door to my right and see a bunch of young girls. I open the door more and let the light into the room. There are no windows or beds or chairs, nothing but four walls and a bucket.

A small whimper comes from a couple of kids in the far corner but besides that they are all silent. I am too far down the hall to even hear Bonney.

I step in the room and eight beautiful women stand up. "Master Harlen, how can we help you?"

"You know who I am?"

"Yes, of course."

"We are all different and are completely happy to serve you in any way you desire."

"Thank you. I truly appreciate it but I'm not ready to choose a wife. If I must, I'm afraid I will leave the decision to Victor."

"I have red hair just like your beloved. Would that please you?"

"I have green eyes. Would that please you?"

"You are all very beautiful but it needs to be more than looks. We had a connection I can't explain."

"Did you love her?"

I think for a moment. "I think if we had anything... I guess it was love. At least I believe it was for me."

Everyone in the room relaxes and slowly moves around the room as if feeling free to move without fear. That's when I notice a young girl of about twelve and a small boy of about four. Wait, Victor said boys were not on high demand and are only brought in on special requests. Oh, God! No! My stomach drops.

I squat down when the two come near me. "Is this your little brother?" I ask the young girl.

She nods.

"How did you both end up here?"

The little boy begins to cry. His big sister cradles his head. It's not your fault Jeremy."

He cries harder. "I'm so sorry, Beffany," he sniffles.

"Can you tell me if anyone said why you are here?" I ask the boy but know it's a long shot.

"Some blonde lady was looking at me, said I would be great for her grandson."

Bonney? "Did the lady say anything about where you're going?"

"No, she said to the big scary man she didn't want me anymore. She said there was no point without her grandson."

"What do you mean?"

The little boy shuts down, afraid because of my frustrated tone.

"I'm sorry. I think that grandson you're talking about is my son. I just want to know where I can find him, please."

The young girl places her hands on the boy's shoulders. "I'm so sorry, but I'm sure I overheard her say there was no point in having a companion if the child was dead."

My blood runs cold. *No, this can't be!* I turn from the room and leave quickly, barrelling towards the fantasy section. As I get closer two security guards open the doors, letting me through.

Halfway down I kick at the door and it cracks, flying open. I don't care that my mother is being ploughed in every way under the sun and they're using anything that a penis could catch friction from like bent arms legs, pressed breasts.

Everyone stops, "Out," I bark.

Victor is sitting behind a desk reading the morning paper as if this was the most natural thing in the world.

"Where is my son?" I ask her.

"Just kill me," Bonney drawls.

"Death is too good for you. I'll make sure this goes on forever if I have to. I'll make your life a bigger hell than you gave me. I swear it."

She tries to hold her head up to talk to me, instead her head falls back. She's too weak to hold it up.

"Is my son dead?" I spit the words, causing Victor to drop his paper and look at us.

Bonney doesn't answer. I move over to the wall and find a cattle prod. I turn it on and jab it into her side. She screams loudly.

"Are you a little more awake now?" I ask her, waving the object in front of her.

"Fuck you!" she spits.

I jab the prod into her back and watch her body shake and scream from all the come so thickly covering her. It's dripping from her, making it even easier to jolt her.

I release the prod and ask again, "Is my son dead?"

"YES! HE'S DEAD!"

I drop the prod. "My son is dead because of you! If he was with me, I would have protected him, and now the only thing of mine and Loralie's is gone."

"You will take a bride and make more." Her tone is cold and lazy.

"You vile bitch! I have nothing left of Loralie at all now, and that's also why you were pushing that I produce another heir. Our baby was stolen from us the moment he was born, never to be touched by us, never to see his face. You never let us know if he was a boy or a girl until this moment when he is dead and buried, and even in death you never allowed us to see him." My tone is low and hoarse as the final walls of my world crash to the ground.

Bonney begins to whimper, "Just kill me."

"Enjoy your time here. It will last long after you have lost your mind, I promise you that."

"No!" she flails, trying to pull herself from the chains holding her. "Fuck you! Fuck you! FUCK YOU!"

"No Bonney, that's what every man in this city is going to do to you," I say, leaving the room as Victor rises and walks after me.

Once we leave the room I give the signal that the room is free to go back to, and sure enough, they all fall into the room and Bonney begins to scream again.

"Are you sure you don't want to just end her now?" Victor asks me.

"Do you have enough men you trust to guard her?"

"Of course I do, but our deal was for her to be dead this night."

"I know but I can't give her what she wants. Your grandson is dead and she won't even tell me how. I need her to suffer as long as you can."

"All right if that is your wish then I'll make it happen. What about you? Have you made a choice for a new bride?"

"I was thinking, would you allow me to choose a family without a bride?"

Victor cocks a brow at me. You have a brother and sister. The boy was going to be Bonney's, but due to the situation he is no longer required, and I know I'll have an easier time if his sister is with him."

Victor looks at me, analysing my words. "From the financial loss of the girl you better leave here with a bride as well or no deal."

"Deal. Pick whatever one you desire as long as I get the two kids too."

"Done."

22

Chapter

I'm actually happy Victor chose a very slim brunette with brown eyes, nothing at all like my Loralie. Within an hour of my return, she arrives at the palace that is my prison, along with the young girl Bethany and her little brother Jeremy who all look overwhelmed and frightened.

I greet them at the foot of the grand polished stairs. "Come with me."

They don't argue or say anything as we walk up the stairs and through the many halls.

"This is the east wing. You will be as free as I can keep you here. I will do my best to make sure you have all you desire."

"I just want my Mummy and Daddy," Jeremy says, lightly tugging at my black suit jacket.

I kneel down to be eye to eye with him. "I can't give you that right now but if I can, I will. If you want to stay safe and not wind up as some sick rich man's playthings, you would all do well to enjoy your freedom here and not push boundaries. I am just as much a prisoner here as you all are. Remember that when you make choices here and note it's my head on the chopping block along with yours."

They all nod solemnly, realizing what I put on the line for them. "Thank you" Bethany says to me with real gratitude in her blue eyes.

"Don't thank me, Bethany. For each of you that I chose, hundreds more were not chosen and they will suffer unimaginable fates."

"Please call me Beth and I heard what was going to happen to me and I saw what those women went through. That fate was going to be mine and most likely my brother's if you didn't do what you did. You couldn't save everyone but you did save us. You might not think it's worth mentioning but three lives are more than none, and my mum always said a single drop of water raises the sea and a single man can make a difference."

I turn my whole body to look at her. This incredible young girl has more wisdom than most her age. "You are wise beyond your years Beth. I think fanning that talent will do you well." I give her a smile and turn to leave.

"WAIT, STOP!" all three of them yell, running after me.

"What on earth is wrong?" I'm a little shook by the sudden outburst.

"Where are you going? Aren't you staying here with us?" Beth asks.

"I was going back to the west wing. As I said before this section will be all yours with as few people to frighten you."

"But I am supposed to be with you. I am to be your wife very soon and they will want a child as soon as I can conceive one for you."

"I'm sorry but I will keep that as far away as I can. I am not ready for anything like that and I will make Victor see that too. So please just try to enjoy your freedom here. You can call for anything, day or night and it will be brought but remember all requests will go through Victor before they are brought here. I expect nothing of any of you." I go to use her name when I realize I don't know it. "You, I don't remember getting your name."

"Oh, I'm so sorry we never did discuss that. I just assumed you would give me one."

"What is wrong with your own?" I ask, a little annoyed.

"I'm sorry. We are not trained to take value with anything, especially our original names."

"I'm sorry. I keep forgetting myself. I just want you to choose a name for me to use."

"Holly."

"Holly it is then," I smile.

Okay, great. Now that introductions are over, I turn and leave before they can stop me again.

Each day is much the same except I no longer eat alone in my office. I now eat at the dining table with Holly and the kids. Beth tells me about all the fun things she did and how she decorated her room, not withholding things she wants for it. I make a mental note for more indoor plants as she seems very fond of them.

Jeremy enjoys telling me about all the new toys he has gotten and what they do. I listen and enjoy seeing them become more comfortable and light up when they talk about something they enjoy, making notes for later.

After dinner, I see them off but not before Holly tries to offer herself to me for the night. I am happy she is not as persistent as Loralie was but she still tries, obviously still afraid of her position here.

I have to admit I have enjoyed the company more than I would care to admit and for the most part. A little viewing each day will show Victor's spies that we are acting like a family.

Work, I would like to say, is much the same but things are getting tighter and tighter with every week that passes. Holly and the kids don't seem to like it when I leave but they have become more at ease over the last month.

Once the hard day is done I like to check in to see how Bonney is doing. She still won't budge on any information and she is hanging in there as much as I have Victor putting her through.

I am far too late today for dinner and everyone else is already in bed so I decide to do the same. By the time I have made it to the west wing a storm has rolled in. I hear the sound of thunder vibrating the ground and the glorious smell when rain hits the ground.

I walk over to a large window in mine and Loralie's room and pull open a white lace curtain with one hand while my other holds a fresh crystal tumbler of bourbon.

I raise the glass and let the liquid burn it's way down as I watch the rainfall and the sky do a light show which I find most peaceful.

Another loud crack of thunder hits, vibrating the ground. The lightning lights up the sky shortly after, showing this storm is almost overhead.

I fasten the curtains up so I can watch the rain from my bed, then remove my pants and shirt, draping them over the chair at my desk that holds my laptop.

Once I'm only in my underwear I climb into bed, between the bourbon and the rain I fall asleep quite easily.

Early the following morning I'm woken up abruptly. My door bursts open, "Jeremy is missing!" Beth and Holly are in my doorway.

I rub my eyes groggily. "This is a huge place. We will find him. What time did he disappear?"

"I fell asleep with him in bed with me. He doesn't like storms at all," Beth says in a panic.

"Okay, so there we have it. He's a little boy afraid of the big storm we had last night. Where would he go?" I go to get up and remember I'm only in my underwear. I see Holly's mouth water a little. Okay, out. Let me put on some clothes and we will find him.

They walk out of the room and give me the time I need. As it is my day off today I grab some jeans and a plain white shirt from my casual drawers, once I close the drawer a groan comes from my bed.

What the fuck? I grab my gun from my side drawer and quickly pull my blankets back to find Jeremy in a ball under the covers still sleeping soundly.

I take a moment to collect myself, disengaging the firearm and returning it to the secret compartment in my side drawer and returning the blankets as they were. I move to the door and open it.

"Great, you're dressed. Can we find my brother now?"

I laugh a little when Beth gives me an irritated look. Wow, she already feels at ease enough to be challenging, or maybe it's just her protective nature for her little brother.

"Jeremy is safe. I found him while I was getting dressed."

Both of them look at me in shock.

"Yeah, looks like the little tike crawled into bed with me at some point in the night. The bed is so big I never even noticed until I was getting dressed."

"Where is he then?"

"I pulled the covers up and let him sleep a little longer."

I hear a little groan behind me and see Jeremy dragging one of my blankets along the floor pinned under one arm that has his thumb in his mouth and the other is rubbing at his eyes.

He sees me and walks over to my leg and wraps himself around my foot before falling asleep again. The poor thing. Obviously 4:30 in the morning is not his wake-up time.

I bend down, gathering him and the blanket in my arms, moving him to the bed. Once I turn to leave, he's awake and at my side again giving the girls a good chuckle.

I sigh, "Okay, this may get difficult in the future. Why can't you sleep in your bed?"

"It's scary. The sky was so scared it cried too!"

I manage to stifle a laugh and smile instead. "The rain will be staying for a few days so why don't you find something fun to do?"

Jeremy just looks up at me with his thumb still in his mouth. Although adorable, I'm sure thumb sucking is bad for their teeth. Oh wow. When did I become this man? I find I'm laughing at myself.

"Will you play with me?"

"I'll make you a deal. You stop sucking your thumb, and I'll do something fun with you."

Jeremy's thumb is out of his mouth quick as lightning with a pop from the break in suction, causing Beth to giggle.

"Okay, whoever wants to join us, I think west wing lounge room." I make a phone call, and by the time we get there everything I have asked for is all set up.

I remember the rainy days with my dad were my favourite. We would play board games and stuff our faces by a warm crackling fire, and when we had enough of games we watched old movies huddled up under a warm blanket with mugs of hot chocolate and giant marshmallows, all the things I have set up for today.

Everyone seems delighted with my idea and we enjoy a rainy day doing just that. It is almost 7 at night and we are in the middle of watching a cowboy movie at Jeremy's request when my phone buzzes.

"I'm sorry, give me a moment," I say, moving Jeremy off my lap where he's been happy most of the day. Once up I move down the hall to my office when I finally answer.

"Victor, what do you need?"

"Nothing my boy, I'm just checking in on you and your new family."

"Oh, well you just called us in the middle of a movie. We've had a great day today."

"Yes I heard. Looks like the world's marshmallow and snack food rocked up at your place today," he laughs.

"If I have my way every rainy day will be this way, so you better look at shares."

"Haha, I believe I will. I'm glad you're enjoying them, but we do have to talk. Things have been getting very hot lately and I'll need you to be very careful. If things keep going the way they are I think it will be best if you came to stay under my roof. You will have just as much privacy as you do now. It just means we can double up security instead of dividing forces."

"Honestly all I need is three men and I promise you I will be safe."

"I'm not willing to take the chance. I hope you will heed my request, I would hate to bring you by force."

I sigh realizing this was never my choice but a demand. "I'll get everything arranged and be there tomorrow."

"Make that immediately. I hate to leave these matters unsatisfied. I have a team downstairs at the main entrance waiting for you now." I hear the phone click and I know the rest is non-negotiable.

I sigh and move to the lounge room. It seems that Victor's men have already come up after us, as they are gone and the room looks like a crime scene.

I know I don't have time to get my things together, not that I don't own anything irreplaceable, so I just go knowing anything I need is already there and that if I leave Holly, Beth, and Jeremy alone with them too long I can't guarantee their safety.

They all run for me when I walk through the doors of Victor's place which is an older version of what I now live in, a huge palace with enough wings and bedrooms to house a small town.

I have Jeremy bundled in my arms before I realize what I'm doing. He visibly relaxes, feeling safer I'm now with him. "I'm sorry. I didn't get to warn any of you. It happened so fast."

"We only just got here but no one is telling us what is going on." Holly looks quite shaken, and I can understand why. This is literally where the devil sleeps, not even I want to be here.

Victor appears at the top of the stairs with his arms opened wide, "Welcome to my happy home. I have arranged for you all to stay in the east wing. Everything you could need is already set up for you. No one will bother you there, but the men are under strict orders to intervene when your safety is at risk. For your continued freedom and safety I do request the three of you don't leave your wing unless with my son or under my orders."

My stomach drops at how much more a person could be imprisoned than before and my biological parents are best at showing me how bad things can always get.

Victor shows us to the east wing which is larger than the west wing at my place where they were staying, but by the end, they were with me most of the time.

"Victor, what is the meaning of all of this?" I ask, cutting to the facts.
"Come with me."

I don't argue. I just do as I'm told and when we walk down the hall to his wing, I pass a hall where I see Lyncon talking to one of the guards. Fuck, he's got my friends here too. Something is definitely wrong.

We turn into his office and Victor sits behind his large, polished, oak desk. He rummages around in his side drawer and pulls out two glasses and a bottle of bourbon.

It irritates me. I finally found where my traits come from. His taste in furniture and use of space, to the bottle of choice in our top desk drawer.

Once filled, Victor pushes the glass towards me. "I know this isn't ideal, but things are getting quite rough out there. Everything is falling apart, but as long as we keep the shipping yard under the highest surveillance, we will get through this."

"I don't understand how a mole from Bonney's team has gotten in with yours. Not even I am privy to a lot of the information to the inner workings."

"Exactly. I have been through everything and I can't find any solid leads that go anywhere. You wouldn't have any ideas, would you Alex?"

"Me? As I said I'm still learning the in's and out's. All of your men seem loyal to you. I have never come across any I would even begin to suspect but I can get Adam, Zac, and Lyncon to help. They have skills that would greatly help."

"Honestly, I already thought that, too. Zac seems to have a great talent for weeding out the rubbish."

"As true as that is, they will not be bullied or contained."

"I wouldn't dream of it. I'll send word for them and get them here to talk out a plan. If I can't get what I need to be done with my men, yours might have better luck right now."

I know even though I'm a little confused right now, he's speaking as if Lyncon and the others are not here, but I'm sure I just saw Lyncon a moment ago.

23

Chapter

It doesn't feel right bringing my friends into this at all. I have done my best to keep them out, but it doesn't seem to stay that way.

Less than half an hour later the guys are all in Victor's office with me. "Wow, long time no see," Zac crosses his arms over his chest, obviously annoyed.

"What could you possibly want with us and here of all places? Victor has finally gotten you hasn't he?" Adam's words feel more disappointed than accusatory.

"Look, I know I haven't been the greatest friend of late and I know I have been acting out of character lately, but I promise there is a reason for everything."

"Yeah, well Victor's men were very forceful in getting us here so this better be good."

"Zac, I know it's not ideal but things have gotten bad. There is someone leaking information and as we fix one issue another one comes at us. Victor needs all of you to help find where it's coming from and help plug it for good."

"I thought you would delight in this being over."

"Adam, you and I both know if this goes down, I am going with it and right now I have Beth, Jeremy, and Holly to think about. They are innocent in all this and if I can get them all back to their homes that would be even better."

"Oh, yeah. I heard you had a replacement family. Heard about that from one of Victor's men. I find it distasteful that I didn't hear it from you."

I screw my nose up at Zac's obvious dig at me. "Since I saw you all last I have imprisoned my mother in a never-ending torture chamber, rescued the only three people from hell that I could, and found out Victor is my father. Everything I love is dying and the last thing I have to lose is the three of you, so forgive me for not wanting to see any of you with a bullet in your heads."

Lyncon steps forward, "Honestly, I'm sexy as sin and could pull off anything but I have to admit I never liked face jewellery."

I crack a smile as Zac and Adam do too. "You never learn that we are brothers. None of us has anything more than each other."

I can't help but realize Adam's meaning since his losing Trin. He only has us. None of us has any family and we have never trusted anyone else to let in as a friend.

"Wait a second! I just mentioned Victor was my father and I've got Bonney being tortured and no one batted an eyelid."

They all look at each other as Zac stuffs his hands in his pockets. "Well you went quiet on us and we wanted to make sure nothing really bad was going on with you so we did what any self-respecting best mates would do, we chipped your phone keys and car."

"You spied on me?"

"Yup."

I shake my head. "Wow I don't know if I should be happy you care about me that much or pissed you trust me so little."

"Um, happy?" Lyncon looks at Zac.

"Yeah, happy sounds good."

"Yeah, we'll go with that," Adam says, picking at a spot on Victor's desk.

I shake my head in amusement at these guys who are the greatest friends a man could ever ask for. "Well, putting everything aside, this is what Victor has brought you in for and he will expect your help. I don't know how we move forward with this one."

Zac moves forward obviously happy with the change of topic. "I have already been looking into all of this. I had a feeling things were not right for a while. Something big started going down within Bonney's ranks a few years ago. After Loralie died things got worse. I found so many leads that went nowhere."

"Victor said the same thing."

"But he didn't have me," Zac says proudly.

"Have you found something?"

"Well I have found quite a few leads that have all led back to a massive company called Prime Industries."

"Prime Industries?"

"Yeah, it gets complicated though. Prime Industries has become one of the biggest companies in the world. There is almost nothing its name isn't connected with, mainstream movies, music, theatre, radio, publishing, restaurants, fashion, you name it. Trying to find the leak is going to take more time than we have."

"What about the CEO of Prime Industries? What can you tell me?"

"Only that he's the biggest phantom I have ever come across. I can't find a thing. Everything is wrapped in so much secrecy not a single whisper has been heard, and when everything went down Prime Industries bought and destroyed everything after the government released it."

"How the hell could they have already released it? These things get held in red tape for years."

"Exactly. These guys are that powerful. I can't even begin to explain how hard this is going to be."

"Give me a list of the information you have so far so I have something to give Victor."

"Wait, you're really going to help Victor? We thought you wanted out? If things go as it looks like they will then we need an exit strategy."

"You don't know what Victor's capable of. By all means, organize an exit strategy if you can but I can't risk Victor thinking I'm hiding anything from him. Especially when all of you are involved and he has Holly and the kids here."

"Speaking of which, I did find the information you wanted of the kids. Unfortunately, if I'm right their family was killed in a house fire. According to records the kids died with them."

I take a moment processing this news. I was hoping I would have a chance to get them all back to their families at some point but find even that is not possible. "Do they have any family at all?"

"Not that I could find. The mother was adopted and the father's parents had died around the same time, father of lung disease and mother they believe of a broken heart."

I clear my throat, pushing the unwelcome tug I feel at the thought. "What did you find on Holly?"

"That's the real interesting one. She has a profile I found alright, perfect and detailed. Perfect English background, wealthy mother and father. She was at the top of all her classes, was accepted into Harvard and was reported missing ten years ago when she never arrived on campus."

"Wow, ten years? That's a long time to be away from your family, but at least we have a good chance of reuniting Holly with her family. What's weird about that?"

"Yeah, it would be good if it wasn't all fake."

I look at Zac, giving him a confused look. "What do you mean fake? Why would she have a fake profile?"

"Good question. It doesn't look like Victor's team set it up either. It looks like it was all in place before she was kidnapped which makes things even weirder."

My head is filled with all sorts of possibilities that all lead to Holly not being who we think she is and what that could possibly mean.

24

Chapter

Victor has not let Zac, Adam or Lyncon go. His need to keep everyone close shows that things are in dire straits right now, but the information about Prime Industries definitely gave them a huge push into Victor's good books.

I have tried to think of how I'm going to breach the conversation with Holly and Victor hasn't helped much with all the work he's given me. Finding time to eat or sleep is hard enough, let alone finding time to have a conversation or to catch up with my friends. The only thing keeping me from losing my mind is knowing my friends are now with the kids so I know they are at least safe for now.

Since all the other sections of Victor's organization have mostly been severed the only one left is the boat yards, making my life a little easier with only having one to look after but harder that this is the end of the line and I'm here most of the time.

I decide to drop in to see Bonney today as I haven't seen her in over a week. Since she has been here I haven't seen much of her, but unfortunately I've been desensitised being here so much, making it only to easy now to be in a room with her while she is naked and being fucked and tortured.

She now has no fingers or toes and her ears have been disfigured without damaging her ability to hear. One eye was carved out with a spoon which I honestly thought she would die from but somehow she has hung in there. I refused the other eye to be removed as I wanted her to be able to see what was happening, and now she is nothing more than a disfigured sex doll.

I move around the room as I watch several old, fat, Asian men fuck her in her widened pussy while a big African man fucks her in the ass. I feel a little discomfort for her when I see him remove himself from her after he's done and find he's hung like a horse. The moment he's out another man takes his place.

She has obviously been fucked so many times she doesn't even make a sound anymore. I look into her swollen face that looks nothing like my mother's anymore. Her eye has not been cleaned well from when she lost her eye and the missing clumps of her hair that have been ripped from her head don't help at all.

Her wrists that are still chained up are not even visible through the vast amount of blood covering the chains. The three old men finish up and let her legs down when they are done with her.

I raise my hand to stop the next lot of guys from coming in and wait for the last guy to finish. As the man before him was obviously bigger it made things difficult for him to finish and instead he just jacks off on her.

Once everyone has left the room I move towards her. The smell is uninviting, a strong stench of come, shit and piss, hers and men that have used her as a toilet. Despite the smell and her disfigured looks, men have still been coming in by the boat loads to fuck, torture, beat and piss on her. Obviously Mr Tanaka was not the only man she pissed off.

"Tell me what happened to my son and I'll make this end now." My voice is soft and gentle.

She raises her head with great difficulty. Her one good eye locks on to me.

"Please tell me. How did my son die?"

A tear trickles down her cheek. "David had watery diarrhea, vomiting and stomach pains for a few days before I picked up something was wrong. When I finally got a doctor in to see him I found that he was too far gone for me to save him."

Her voice is cracked and raspy so I walk away to the corner of the room and get her a glass of water. When I return I put the cool glass to her dried cracked lips. She tries to drink faster than her starved throat would allow, causing her to cough.

"I wanted so badly to have a second chance of being a mother and I failed. David died because I dared to love him." Her words sound true and remorseful. "I was so wrapped up in getting what I wanted I didn't look at what I had until it was too late. After that I didn't know how to be anything else. I thought with another child with my blood was the closest I would get."

I listen to her intently as she struggles to get each word out and when she stops I give her a sip of water, urging her to tell me more.

"Once David's skin changed in colour and thickness I knew there was something seriously wrong. That's when I found out he had been poisoned with arsenic. At first I thought someone was trying to kill him but after he had died at the hospital I had come back home to find a large amount of my servants missing. That's when I was grabbed and quickly brought back here when they found out one of the plants we owned was being investigated for high levels of arsenic in the drinking water. It never touched me because I never drank tap water and the very power I fought to get killed my second chance and sent every agent to my front door." Her eyes water and I know it's the truth. "Since Frank was already dying I knew there was not much they could do to imprison him so I used Frank to get out and came back here but some company had written an affidavit exonerating him of all wrongdoings, forcing me on the run. But that didn't last long, now did it?" She tried a dry chuckle causing her to cough. "I've told you everything. Please put me out of my misery," she begs.

I move to the far wall and find the hose. I turn it on and let the water flow over her, washing all the body fluids from her. After she is cleaned I wrap a clean towel around her and move to her shackles and release them. The blood has dried on to the cuffs causing her wounds to open up when I pull them free. She doesn't cry or flinch but she does draw in a breath when her arms are let down.

Besides the times she is held up so she can be fucked, this is the only time in the last two weeks that she has had her arms down. Obviously the feeling is overwhelmingly good.

Her legs don't have the strength to hold her, so I let her down gently to the floor as I sit with her, cradling her body. I feel her hand stagger up to mine that holds her waist.

My body goes stiff at the thought of what she is trying to do. Even though she is beyond damaged I still don't trust her. When her hand settles on mine I get confused.

"I can feel you tensing. I really did mess up for you to hate me so, didn't I? In my last moments can't you just pretend you loved me for even a moment?"

"But I did love you."

She scoffs.

"I did. I wanted nothing more than to please you. I had hoped one day I would make you smile the way you smiled for others but you never did, not once. After I watched everyone I ever got close to die or disappear I lost hope that day would ever come."

"Do you remember the dog you made me out of clay in primary school?"

"Yes, you said it looked more like a pig than a dog and had more luck turning into bacon than into something worth treasuring."

"I did say that, didn't I? That reminds me, when I die please cremate me and wherever you throw me can I at least be with my most prized treasure please. In the family vault behind the back red curtain you will find a glass cabinet on a red velvet pillow you will find it. I know I don't deserve anything from you, but please if you could find it in your heart, I really .....do love ... you." Her hand slips from mine. Her chest no longer rises and falls, her body going limp.

"Goodbye Mum." It gets to me that in her last moments she was more of a mother to me than she was my entire life.

After a few moments I finally rise to my feet, taking her body with me. I open the door and find Doug and Theo are at the door. Theo holds out his arms to me, offering to take my mother's body.

I hold her for a moment longer and know I have to let go. "Can you take care when cremating her? And I want her ashes please." Theo nods his head acknowledging my request and Doug does the same.

Once they are out the door my phone vibrates in my pocket. I retrieve it and read the message.

Get out now.

A cold chill runs down my spine, but I don't waste time when a second one follows shortly after.

Get out now! They are coming.

I am barely out the gate and down the road when what looks like the entire police force is screeching into the shipping yard.

My heart is racing at how close they were from finding me there. Who the hell sent me the message and how did they know and why did they warn me?

25

Chapter

The drive back is fast considering my mind is racing with so many thoughts and questions. I have always done as I was told and never really thought to ask questions.

I have tried to call Adam, Zac and Lyncon but no one is answering, giving me even more to think about.

Victor said all the underground facilities were in no way connected to us at all which gives me a little breathing space the further I drive away from the shipping yard.

Victor always said the shipping yard was the closest guarded secret because as long as it stayed safe all the rest could fall and it wouldn't damage the organization.

Now it's in the hands of the government. All those girls are now safe but Victor is going to be hard to handle once he finds out about this and I don't want Holly, Beth and Jeremy copping what comes next.

I turn into the driveway and gladly find it empty of visitors or cops, remembering again it had no way to be traced back to Victor and yet I still feel uneasy.

I quickly park and run up the stairs, taking them two at a time and leaving my car door open in the rush.

"HOLLY! BETH! JEREMY!"

I yell each of their names hoping to hear something. I check in every room looking for them. Not even a servant is around which starts to worry me even more.

"VICTOR! Where the hell is everyone?"

I give up on the house and run out the front doors and back to the car. Once I get there I see a black Mercedes block my 1962 Ferrari 250 GTO in, stopping me from moving. The back window goes down revealing Victor in the back seat.

"What's going on? Where is everyone?"

"I was about to ask you the same thing."

I freeze, staring at him. "You don't know where Holly and the kids are?"

"No, I came back and found no one here so I sent everyone off to look for Holly and the kids. We can't afford to have them on the loose, especially right now when things are very rocky."

I think for a moment he's talking about all this as if he has no idea about the shipping yard, which means he had no part in sending that message to get me out of there before they hit.

"Get in. We will look together," he says, opening the back door to let me in. I feel uneasy about this but I get in anyway.

Victor seems pleased, showing me something is definitely wrong and I somehow saved myself in some way. I notice his left hand in his pocket relaxes and retreats to rest on the luxury leather arm rest at his side, confirming my suspicions I just dodged a bullet in the literal sense.

"What's going on Victor?" I ask him with my most no nonsense voice I can muster.

He looks at me and decides to trust me with whatever is going on. "I will release you from any marital contracts and sign the kids over to you legally as long as I get Holly."

There it is. Holly and whatever her fake profile means has been uncovered and I was just tested to see if I had any part in it.

"Holly's our spy, isn't she?"

"It does look that way but all the pieces don't fit. She was at the learning centre for the last ten years. She had no way of knowing she would be taken and she had no way of contacting anyone outside those walls."

"I had a similar issue after Zac told me."

Victor doesn't say anything so my hunch Zac gave him this information was correct with my back up. This seals Zac's trustworthy and usefulness, which for now keeps them alive.

"After the information Zac found we managed to pick up his leads and found Holly's true file. The whole thing was way too professionally done, so we went digging and found her real profile. It looks like she is an undercover agent."

"What? How is that possible? She was taken at a very young age and she has been here for ten years. That's a long time for an agent."

"Yes, I thought of all those things too. It looks like they set up a sting operation that went horribly wrong. We broke into the archives and found the mission was terminated after the bust went wrong. It looks like they were after someone else and we picked up the agent before they had a chance because of the security sweep. Any chance of her being tracked from any device on her clothes or body would have been taken from her within moments of her being grabbed."

I swallow hard, realising he means they are stripped and raped before they even get to the yard. I am so glad the horror pit is gone and if I go with it, good riddance. I deserve anything I get for the things I have done to survive and the more he's talking the more I believe no one has even called to tell him what's happened.

"Honestly it is sounding more and more like she couldn't possibly be the spy – just in the wrong place at the wrong time."

"Yes, it does look that way but we can't be too careful."

I nod automatically, giving him the answer he wants.

"How was things today?"

I swallow and decide to give the short truth. "The new batch of girls came in and the ones for Chase Hunter went out to that massive island of his. Do you know what he does with them?"

"I never ask questions. I just deliver."

"Yeah but to have large quantities on regular basis for big girls just seems off."

Victor laughs, "If anything has taught you that people have fucked up fantasies, I thought the fantasy room and the learning centre would have taught you that."

He's right. Out of all the things to find strange I pick that of all things. I push the thought aside when Victor asks "Did you see Bonney today?"

"Yes I did," I reply solemnly.

Victor fills a crystal tumbler with ice and bourbon and raises it to his lips, sipping the amber liquid. "She sure is a pathetic creature nowadays."

"If I didn't know any better I would think you felt sorry for her."

"No matter what Alex, she is the mother of my son and I will always have a place in my heart for her for that, but I promise you I feel nothing more for the woman. I was only stating a fact."

He takes another sip. I clear my throat. "Then it won't matter to you that it's over. She died today. Moments before I left she was taken to the incinerator. Doug and Theo said they would be by later to deliver her ashes."

Victor stills for a moment, taking in the news. Then he finishes his glass in one big gulp and refills it again, "Bullet?"

"No, she succumbed to her injuries."

Victor gives a light laugh, "You have to hand it to her. She was a tough one to crack." He waives his glass. "This is to you Bonney. May you find in death what you never found in life."

I pour myself a glass just the same minus the rocks and clink my glass to his. "To Bonney."

We drink in silence for a small moment. "When I get the kids back I want your blessing to go somewhere and wait for things to cool off."

Victor's head snaps to me. "I need you here more than ever. Things are not safe at all. There is nothing left except the shipping yards. As long as we have those we will get back on track."

"This company Prime Industries is snatching up everything that is getting taken from us. They took all Bonney's and they are taking every-thing of yours, no matter how small. However they are involved, it's on a big scale. That is where we need to be looking. Put some safety money away, shut down and run."

"You're telling me to run off with my tail between my legs? I am Victor Alexander Bright. I don't run. They run from me."

I exhale deeply knowing his pride is going to destroy us all. I'm about to tell him about the shipping yard when we come to a stop outside the palace I was given to live in to find it completely surrounded by law enforcement.

"Go," the moment the word is out of Victor's mouth into the small speaker on his door.

"Yes sir." And then we are off.

"Looks like we need to head straight for the airport. Forget Holly and the kids. Looks like we need to go now."

I'm grateful for him to leave them alone and take my advice but I'm also worried. If Victor didn't take them then where the hell are they and are they safe?

Victor makes a few phone calls and after each one he is furious when none of them answer. "What the fuck is going on? Where is everyone?" He dials another number and this one answers immediately.

"You got something for me? I need a magic carpet fast. Yep. Yep. Ahuh. Perfect. Be there in ten." He puts the phone down in a more controlled manner than before. Obviously he just got good news.

"Private air strip on smith and vine."

"Yes sir," the little speaker replies.

Immediately the limo changes direction.

"Air strip? don't you think that will be a little obvious?"

"Not at all. Some big boy band just cancelled their flight last minute. It leaves to return to Texas in twenty minutes after refueling."

I have to admit it would be a good cover flight. Although we still would not be able to be on the flight as a passenger until we are in the air.

As we get closer to the airport luckily Victor has not heard about the ship yards. Honestly I was dreading him finding out, but thankfully no one has answered their phones. As soon as we rock up to the airstrip several officers are on the tarmac. The limo slows then turns quickly, leading us in the opposite direction.

Victor grabs the car phone and begins to smash it repeatedly on the small table in front of him. Once he has calmed down and I'm officially on the sharpest edge of my life.

Victor speaks into the speaker again, "Albatross?"

"Gone sir."

Victor growls through his teeth. "Sumarra?"

"Gone sir."

"Shipping yard beta."

"Yes sir."

Victor visibly relaxes at his driver's reply. Once at the beta yard which has nothing but imports and exports come through here, it has no negative paper trail at all, which makes it a good choice.

We get to the yard and the gates open immediately. Once we are in we move right to the end of the dock where the ship awaits. The moment Victor and I are out of the limo it begins to reverse off the dock and out of sight. We are up the ramp and on the deck in no time. Victor grabs for the door and opens it to go inside.

"I'm sorry, Victor. I can't go with you."

He freezes at my words. "We have a contract boy. You do as I say. You gave yourself to me willingly. Don't be foolish."

"This has nothing to do with you and me or any stupid contract. I need to find my friends and I need to find Holly and the kids. Everything is falling apart and I have to stay and try and salvage what I can." I hope my bullshit concern for the company saves me from being shot for my insolence.

"Alexander, I don't give a shit about anything else but your safety. Get in and forget everything else. You can make new friends, adopt all the kids you like and help me build far stronger than before."

I stand taller and more defiant than I ever have in my life. "I said no."

26

Chapter

"No? You're telling me no?"

"Your contracts are not worth a damn and if they are found, I am best gone anyway. There is no reason for me to follow you now. Everything is gone. This is my chance to find something real."

"Like Loralie? You think that was real? You think that even if Loralie was alive she would love you?" Victor scoffs, "No one in your life cares about you without my say so."

That is it. My heart is broken, obliterated into a billion pieces. Any last vestiges of hope are completely gone. Lyncon, my friend, my brother, steps out, walking over to stand at Victor's side.

I don't understand. I don't believe it! No, this is wrong! I know Loralie loved me and I know Lyncon would never hurt me. We are brothers.

Victor seems to have made his point. The look on my face I can't hide and Victor is claiming his victory with a huge grin on his face.

I try to shake off this feeling I have. "Lyncon, what is the meaning of this?" I ask, stepping towards them.

Instantly and without a word, Lyncon has his gun trained on me, stopping me instantly. I look at Victor and scowl.

He only laughs at me. "This is only to teach you an important lesson, boy. Everyone is under my control. Every secret you hold is mine and if you stop fighting me I will give you this same power."

I sneer at Victor and take a defiant step.

Bang!

Lyncon fires a shot Infront of my foot in warning. I look at him trying to get a read from one of my closest and dearest friends but he gives nothing away. His eyes are cold and mechanical.

Shit, if this is true then I am fucked. Lyncon knows everything. He knows all of my secrets. If that is the case then I have nothing. Victor wins.

He said everyone closest to me is under his control. Does that mean Adam and Zac are under his control too?

I would give anything to go back even to last week when my friends and I enjoyed a laugh. Those times couldn't have been fake. They felt real to me.

I take another step.

Bang!

Another warning shot from Lyncon.

"We are brothers Lyncon. I trust you with my life. I love you like my own flesh and blood. I would give everything for you. I don't believe you would betray me like this."

I take another defiant step.

Bang!

Without hesitation or feeling in his cold eyes, he fires again. This time I feel the bullet sink into my left shoulder.

Victor laughs wickedly. "Such devotion to your friend but he is not yours. He will shoot you with every step closer to me you take. Stop this now. Let things go back to what they were Alexander, the days where you both were friends will still be as they were. Nothing needs to change."

"But they were not real! I want something real in my life! This bullet wound may be that, a bullet in my body but it is real and I am starting to think it is the only real thing I have ever gotten."

I step again.

Bang!

My left leg faults as he shoots a bullet into my thigh. Victor's demeanour changes. I think by this time he had hoped I would have changed my mind and come back to him.

I go to take another step.

Click.

I hear the sound of a gun being engaged ready to fire but it isn't Lyncon's. *No!* My eyes go wide as I watch Victor raise his gun to Lyncon's head.

"If you will not come back to me by choice I will do it by force."

"Why should it matter to me if you kill them all? You said so yourself, they don't give a fuck about me. It was all a game and I fell for it hook, line and sinker."

"Just because they have been trained to take my every order without question, it doesn't mean you can't have them with you like before. Any blood spilt from this moment on is in your control and will be on your hands."

He's desperate. I know that he is scared. The company is falling apart and I am his one and only blood heir. Even though I know all that, I don't dare take another step.

"Come back with me," Victor commands, hope flooding his words.

I look at my hands. The amount of blood shed from these hands is off the charts. I have barely gotten through without selling another human being or destroying an innocent life but if I go with him now, that will be it. I will end up one of his trained robots and there will be nothing that could save my soul.

I would rather die. Loralie taught me how to love and feel love in return. If she was under his control like he says then why would she steer me away from what Victor obviously wanted? If it was a test then she would have been stopped long ago, right?

I can't think straight. I am overloaded. My heart is broken and yet I am holding on to the tiniest pieces with everything I have left.

My brain is trying to reason with everything I know to be true up until now, but I keep coming up empty handed. I have nothing left. I have two choices: join Victor and do untold damage I will never recover from, or die by the hand of one of my best friends or my father. This is so fucked up.

I have made up my mind. I would rather die than give my gun to the devil. I take that next step fast, heading right for Victor. Lyncon shoots me in the chest. I feel it hit, winding me but nothing more. I keep running. Victor pulls the trigger.

Bang!

Lyncon drops to the floor. I don't stop. I keep running towards him. Victor turns his gun on me.

Bang!

Bang!

Two shots are fired and Victor goes down. I stop and look behind me. Adam and Zac are standing there with guns raised, ready to die for me.

Tears are threatening my eyes at the sight. They are not Victor's, they are mine. I can see it on full display, giving me a little of my heart back.

I run to Lyncon, blood gushing from his neck from where victor shot him. "Fff...lllass b..book." Lyncon tries to say something to me but he can't get the words out properly before his body goes limp.

Bang!

Bang!

Another two shots are fired and Adam and Zac dive for cover.

Victor is pulling himself up, the front of his clothes drenched in his blood.

My blood boils as he fires at my friends again.

I launch myself at him. Before he has a chance to turn his gun on me I am on him. I knock his gun from his hand and my hands are around his throat. I dig my fingers in with everything I have, all of the betrayal, hurt, loss. I put everything I have left into attacking him.

He claws at my hands, desperate to be free of me but I am so enraged nothing will save him now. My thumb is the first to sink into his throat, then another finger until I push through the back, hooking behind the soft tissue.

"This ends now! I will never be anyone's puppet. I will never marry or have kids. Your line dies with me, and as for your precious company, the head of the snake is being chopped as we speak. Your reign is over. You are nothing and your name and fortune is gone. I wanted you to know before I send you to hell where you belong."

His eyes go wide, fear finally shaking this unshakable man. I dig my thumb in all the way and pull as hard as I can. I feel his throat give way to my strength as it rips from his body, blood pumping from the hole I have just made.

I stand up quickly as his eyes show me everything I have always wanted to see in this man, that his life is just as fragile as any other, that he bleeds like any other and that even the devil can be killed. He is a man like any other.

I never noticed before but as I stand there watching the life drain from my father I feel myself slipping. I feel nothing. This man helped bring me into this world. I should feel something for him, right?

But I feel nothing but relief as he takes his last breath, no bells, no fireworks, no lights, nothing. He's just gone. Dead on the ground. I just continue to stand there holding a portion of his throat in my hand.

27

Chapter

"What was it that Lyncon was trying to say to you?" Zac asks.

"Something about a las book."

"What the fuck does that mean?" Adam asks.

I think about his words. He was desperate for me to know whatever it was.

"Well...book is easy. Let's start with the fact that books are usually found in a library."

"Yeah, that is not easy when all of Victor's properties are being raided as we speak."

"Wait, he was trying to say something that started with 'F.'"

"Like fuck you?" zac smirks.

I roll my eyes at him. I felt nothing when Victor died but I did for Lyncon. I feel it in the pit of my stomach.

F... When I think of books I think of my father. My head shoots up.

"Frank."

"What?"

"Frank. What if he was trying to say 'Frank's book?"

"He has thousands of books. That would be like looking for a needle in a haystack," Zac remarks with a sigh.

My father did try to make sure that when our family fortune fell the house that was once his parents was in no way connected to anything they could take. It was supposed to be the one safe place no one could take from me but I guess he underestimated Bonney.

I have only been back once since my mother killed him in his favourite place in the world, right in front of my eyes.

We rock up to the mansion. The massive hole in the side where the bomb went off is now covered in tarps and plastic to protect what they can. Besides that there is no sign of anything else.

I hear the car doors slam and Adam and Zac are right at my side. "We are right here."

"Yeah man, we've got this," Zac says, placing a hand on my shoulder.

"You don't have to come with me," I say, stronger than I feel.

"Nah man, we have had enough time away. This we do together," Zac says, finalising the argument.

I take one last breath and walk up the grand stairs and into the massive double doors. The polished wood creaks from the lack of up-keep as it opens.

All of the debris has been cleaned up and sealed off and repairs had begun before the whole organization began to take a huge hit.

We walk into the house I grew up in. I walk past old paintings of my mother's side of the family. It isn't until we get to the back heading into my father's wing that I notice the paintings stop and photos of me growing up line the hall.

I don't remember these. I look at a picture of me throwing leaves around the courtyard with a gleeful look on my face as I run away from the gardener who is chasing me with a rake.

Adam chuckles, "I like this one."

I'm about to say 'me too' when I realise he is not looking at the one I am. This is a picture that hits me hard. It is a picture of Adam, Zac, Lyncon and I. We went on a training camp that ended up being one of my greatest memories.

In this photo Lyncon and I are charging for Zac and Adam's hill flag as Adam trips Zac who has the flag as they run from us. I smile, letting the memory flood my thoughts. I remember this.

Adam says with a laugh, "Great. We need to burn this picture. My mouth is wide open," he grumbles.

"Don't you dare. None of these pictures are ever being touched. These are my father's treasures." You can see the care in each and every one as it was placed and framed.

We walk a little further and there is a picture of Adam and I at the age of twelve on horses. The next photo is of Zac in a headlock with Lyncon looking at the camera with the biggest grin on his face. We all look at it, missing a piece of ourselves.

The next photo is a happy, light hearted picture of the four of us laughing with our arms draped over each other's shoulders. I begin to move when I see something. Right in the back is Loralie peeping out from behind a tree.

What the fuck?

I look closer and sure enough, it is her. There is no mistaking it. This picture was taken only a few months ago. It was the first time I laughed after Loralie died.

Zac is the first to notice what has me so transfixed, "No way!"

"What is it?" Adam asks, pushing in front of Zac. It isn't until Zac points her out that Adam notices. It is super easy to overlook. I almost did too.

"How is this possible? This is just before Frank died. In fact, I think this was the last photo he took of us before he died. Loralie was supposed to have died eight months before this photo was taken.

Loralie is alive.

I go back and look through all the pictures again but don't see any other pictures with her in them. I get to the end of the hall where I find the grand door to my father's library.

I stop, hovering my hand over the door handle before gathering the courage to open the door. I take a deep breath and open the door.

The library is huge and well-lit. There are stairs and balconies all around the room, and right in the middle is my father's chair, side table, overhead light and reading magnifying glass all set up like they are waiting for him to come in at any moment and pick up a book.

I hear Zac sigh from my left. "This is going to take forever. It looks bigger than I remember if that is at all possible."

Adam places a hand on his shoulder. "Give me books instead of a gun fight any day. Come on, we have a lot to get through." Adam goes up a set of stairs to my left and Zac goes to the back of the library to the right and I head straight for my father's chair.

The last time I was here I watched my father die right here in this spot in my arms. The whole area is clean without one thing out of place.

I sit in his chair, the one place I never dared to sit. This thrown was so unreachable to anyone but him.

The chair is soft and comfortable, and for the first time I look up and see everything from his perspective.

The door is right in front of me across the room. There is no way he could have missed Mother at the door with a gun on him.

He knew. I remember how he held my head. He was protecting me, making sure he didn't move in case it hit me instead. Tears threaten my eyes. I move my hand to his little side table and find the book he was in the process of reading before he died.

I freeze when I take in the book more closely. This was the *last* book he was reading. What if Lyncon was trying to say 'Frank's last book'? It would make so much sense.

No one would think to disturb his final place, no one but me, that is. I hover my hand over the book for a fraction longer then lift it from the table.

Once in my lap I see the title, *Secrets From the Grave by E.G. Never*. This is that huge author that has the world on end. Secrets From the Grave, how fitting for a last book.

The book mark I made for him when I was five is right at the back with only a few pages left to finish E.G. Never's final story.

I ignore the bookmark, leaving it in place as I read the first few pages. My eyes grow wide.

"Zac! Adam!"

They both bolt out towards me, dropping whatever they were doing and run to me, guns in hand.

They both look around then at me. "What is it?" they both ask in hushed voices.

"Guns away. Find where all the E.G. Never books are."

They both put their guns away hesitantly, but Adam speaks first. "I saw 'E' down this way. He has everything by author, not book title." That does not surprise me at all. Adam leads Zac to the section he indicated, and sure enough, they return with over forty books between them.

"Okay, now what?" Zac asks.

"Put them in order from the first release to last and begin reading," I say.

"What is this torture?" Zac grumbles. "I would rather shoot someone."

I roll my eyes at him but just like Adam, Zac is riveted from the first page just like the rest of us and they both know why.

Not only are these books incredibly written but each and every story is our stories, the stories of our family. Each and every book is one of our adventures made into a best seller with all the information on how each bad guy was defeated.

This is how the police got all of the information. This is how they found out everything. Whoever wrote these is someone close to us. Whoever wrote these is someone I trust. There are too many things in here that are things only Victor and I knew and some only I knew. The only other person I ever told about these things was Loralie.

The last story E.G Never wrote was the story of the young girl who fell in love with the son of the devil and that love cost her dearly. It cost her, her freedom. She was tortured, beaten and raped. This is Loralie's story of how she survived the training and how she watched as child after child was put into her and she emotionlessly watched them be taken. My heart bleeds as she gives all of herself in such a way no one could believe it was true, just an incredible story about an angel falling into the hands of the devil and eventually fed to the devil's beast of a son who she falls deliriously in love with. My heart skips a beat when I read her struggles with her heart and her mission.

For her to escape she had to fake her death to protect her love from afar and this is how she did it.

s she touched.

28

Chapter

This gives all the information one would need to crush both organizations and it did. I'm feeling ambivalent. If this is all true, Loralie is still alive and she loves me, but it could also be the fluff. This E.G. Never needed to make a good story.

I jump slightly when I hear the doorbell ring. Who the fuck is calling here of all places? I get to the security room and see the police are at the front door. Not wanting to lose my place in the book, I walk with my finger inside, marking my place. I take a breath and answer, hoping if they arrest me at least I'll have a book to while away the hours.

Three officers stand before me, dread washing over me. I only hope they will take me and leave Zac and Adam alone.

"Alexander Harlen, I presume?"

"Yes." Wow, that came out way calmer than I thought was possible.

"It is an honour to meet you." All three officers lift their caps in respect.

What the fuck? I am so confused. It obviously shows.

The officer in the front gives a little laugh, "I am sorry. I know you wanted to stay anonymous but without all your help we couldn't have accomplished such a feat. As hushed as we can we wanted to thank you and deliver your papers in person."

I reach my hand out and take the large envelope. Once it is in my hand they all stand to attention and salute me, turn, and leave.

I watch the gates close behind them before I return to the library so confused. Zac and Adam look at me with concern.

"What's got you making a face like that?

"Well he hasn't been arrested so that's a good thing, isn't it?"

They both look at me.

" I just got saluted by a bunch of police officers and given paperwork I requested apparently."

I grab the bookmark and put it in the book so I can put it down, freeing my hands to open the large A4 envelope.

Inside are several documents. First, I pull the deed to my dad's house out. I cannot begin to express how happy I am to have this in my hands. Along with it is a letter.

To Mr Alexander Harlen,

It is with great pride that we close the case of the Harlen and Bright family Run organizations with great success.

As discussed, your father's home has been returned. Enclosed is the deed to fourteen Calem parade fort Maren. Your country and myself wish to thank you for your sacrifices and involvement. Enclosed are the documents outlining the agreement between you and the government.

As discussed, also enclosed are the only files left in existence on you and Mr. Zac James Branthem and Mr. Adam Judas Simons.

These are yours to do with as you please. Once again, I would like to extend my thanks.

Regards,

Judith Whitman

"Oh my god, isn't that the president?"

"Yep, sure is. I don't understand. We have been exonerated from all parts played and given second chances with clean records and given all the credit for something we had nothing to do with. What the fuck is going on?"

Adam and Zac take each of their files and begin to read.

"Holy shit! These guys are thorough. They have the report in here that Ms. Veldan filed when I drove her car into the neighbour's pool."

"Haha! I remember that she was so mad until Dad bought her a new car and replaced the fencing. Oh that takes me back."

I can't help but laugh at some of the silly things in each of our files. "What are you both going to do with your files?" I ask, them putting mine into the fireplace.

Both Zac and Adam join me by the fire and do the same. "New beginning," Adam mumbles.

"Yeah, new beginning," Zac repeats.

"I still have no idea how this is all happening," I admit.

"Well, we still have more reading to do. Let's see if we find anything. I'm on my last book. What about you?"

"Yeah, me too," I say, picking up the book and waving it in the air when a folded piece of paper falls out.

I bend down and retrieve the piece of paper and unfold it. Instantly I find myself sinking into my father's chair, completely shaken.

Hey Alex, if you're reading this then things went as I thought they would and I'm not there with you. First, if you killed me, fuck you. If Victor did, which is most likely, I hope you killed the mother fucker. (See what I did there? Mother fucker because he fucked your mother. Haha! Dead and still sharp as ever, not to mention devilishly handsome and sexy as sin.

Getting to the point, all of this played out like we thought it would. I have been working for Victor since I was a boy. He made me into everything you would want in your inner circle. I never knew any better and I hope you believe that.

I'm responsible for a lot of shit in your life so I decided I was gonna go out with a bang most likely literally.

Frank, Willow, and I are Prime Industries. Frank started it years ago as a way to protect his legacy and you in an emergency. Once Willow and I joined in it started to become a way to make things right and break our cages.

Together Frank and Willow created E.G Never, the perfect revenge. No really, that's what it says backwards. Clever if I do say so myself. That beautiful bride of yours came up with it. I spoke with a few men in Victor's palace that helped with minor things like killing Loralie so Willow could flourish.

Once I was given the hit I had to save what I could but I also had to make it look like I was doing my job to stay in high regard to Victor.

All I ever wanted was for the only family I ever had to be happy. Acting the fool can only go so far. So this is my gift to all of you, the gift of freedom. So now go be happy, all of you.

Your loving brother Lyncon

P.s

He is gonna keep you on your toes

P.P.S

Adam is gonna want to kiss me and kill me but to late for both so fuck ya haha!

I know a tear is trickling down my face but I don't care. He was my brother all along, and still crazy as ever.

"Hey, what does he mean by I'll want to kiss him and kill him?"

"I want to know who this guy is that's going to keep me on my toes."

I look down at the book and notice the last page of the book has a single paragraph.

This story doesn't have a real ending. The reason for that is, it has yet to be written. At some point the main character of my story will eventually read this and realize there is a happy ending waiting for him in the place we found freedom, happiness and each other.

My head shoots up, "Let's go."

I race out the door and stop when I remember I don't have my Ferrari anymore. Zac pulls his keys out and presses a small remote to my father's garage on his keys, revealing his truck. I shake my head.

"Shut the fuck up. If you want to get there, get in the truck."

Not wanting to waste another moment, I climb into the massive black truck that has more in common with a monster truck than a normal truck. Once we are all belted in Zac is off. He's enjoying himself way too much and I have difficulty giving directions and keeping my stomach contents in place. After a far shorter time with Zac driving we manage to find the overgrown driveway.

Once on the road, Zac creeps up the driveway carefully. Although anyone could most likely hear us a mile away.

The clearing comes into view and the cherry blossoms appear. Holy shit. They are in full bloom. Beautiful pink blossoms fill the long road with vibrant colour reminding me of the blossoms in Japan.

The arches are full and luscious with Jasmin that permeates the scenes making the whole experience breathtaking.

We reach the massive water feature with the loving couple in an embrace and that's when I see her. Under the large willow tree reading a book is my Loralie.

I move out of the truck, and it seems Zac and Adam are in shock or just don't want to disrupt this moment and I'm glad because I can't think of anything but this glorious moment.

Loralie sees me. She drops her book and pulls herself off the grass, gathering her white cotton dress so she can run to me.

Our arms fly around each other as our mouths crash together. The kiss is wild, hungry, desperate, and messy and the best kiss of my life.

"Loralie I –."

She places a finger to my lips stopping me. "First, Loralie is dead. My name is Willow, and second," she looks around me to see Zac and Adam in the truck.

She grins widely. She steps back from me and whistles between her two fingers. A few minutes later Adam is out of the truck and bolting across the gravel and down the grass to Trinity in a beautiful red dress with yellow sun flowers on it.

Adam crashes into her so hard he knocks her off her feet, tumbling to the ground in a heap. I pull Willow to me, holding her tightly as we watch them cry and fall apart over each other. I turn to look at Willow, my heart bursting, "I love you Willow."

She smiles brightly, "Say it again."

"I love you," I laugh.

"No, the part where you said my name."

I grin. "I love you Willow."

She nuzzles her head into my chest, savouring the moment. I look over to see Trinity and Adam are gone and Zac has started up his truck. He gives me a happy wave and I give one back before he drives back down the driveway, obviously not wanting to disturb the couple renewals.

"I think Adam and Trin have the right idea," I say, pulling her to me seductively. She giggles and pulls away as I hear two voices squeal out the backyard. I move closer to the sound. The closer we get the more I feel Willow stiffen.

The moment I turn the corner a small boy no older than one slams into my legs and falls backwards. He doesn't cry. He just stares at me. I shake off my surprise and reach my hand down to him. He takes it tentatively.

Once the boy is back on his feet I ask, "What's your name son?" He doesn't reply.

I look at Willow. She smiles as a little girl in a pink princess dress and pigtails ploughs into the little boy, knocking him to the ground again. Willow laughs, picking them up off the ground and dusting them off.

"Alex, meet your daughter Hope and your son Lyncon."

My heart stops. For the first time in my life I'm completely shocked and lost as to how to handle this. My hands begin to shake at my sides, so I shove them in my pockets.

Little Hope is the first to come up to me but Lyncon shoves in front of her.

"Nice to meet you Lyncon. I love your name."

He smiles, showing all his teeth.

Lyncon said it in his letter. I now know the 'he' he was referring to and I don't doubt he's right. This little guy is going to definitely keep me on my toes.

I lift Hope and Lyncon into my arms and hold my twin babies. I'm a dad and Willow and Trinity are alive. I laugh as I realize why Lyncon said Adam would want to kill him and kiss him because of his involvement with Trinity's death and keeping her safe for him. He said in his letter he was given a hit to carry out and had to save what he could without losing standing with Victor. This is two of those very moments he broke the rules and set them free for us to find when it was safe. We walk into the house that was once our safe haven and now is our future, a bright and happy one we choose for ourselves.

It's been a year since everything fell apart. E.G Never's book is still a bestseller. I found Holly held up with the kids in an old safe house.

Willow fell in love with them the moment she saw them and now they are officially ours. Willow is pregnant again making our large home full of love and laughter.

Holly is back on the force and comes to visit often which the kids love as well.

Adam and Trin tied the knot in a small ceremony under the blossom trees at the manor a few days after we found the girls and are now expecting their own baby boy.

Argus is back with me and is enjoying his new security detail as the children's guard. It's a very quiet job and I have never seen Argus so stress free and happy. Seeing him with the kids is the happiest I have ever seen him.

He is so laid back now he even let's Hope do his hair which looks surprisingly good in bows and glitter.

As for Zac, we haven't seen him since he left but he does check in from time to time, letting us know he's doing all right. The last I heard from him he was cleaning up some loose ends from the businesses and even met a nice girl, although he was very sketchy on the details.

In the end, life couldn't be better. Lyncon and Hope love chasing each other around the house. The amount of fights these two get into is incredible and the better they get on their feet and the more they talk the louder the house gets which I love.

While lost in my happy thoughts, Lyncon is tackled into the metal fireplace cage by Hope who is surprisingly strong for a little girl, knocking Bonney's urn off the mantle. I manage to dive and catch it before any damage is done.

Both stop, frozen at what they have done. I get up and brush myself off as I place Bonney back on the mantle where she has watched over her grandkids.

I think back to our last moments together and remember something Bonney asked me to do. As luck would have it, Argus comes through the door.

"Hey Argus, could you take over for a bit and tell Willow I'll be home late and she will be able to reach me on my mobile?"

"Long trip?"

"I'm just going back to Dad's. I need to look for something."

" Do you want me to give Adam and Trin a heads up that you're coming?"

"No. I'll do that on the way there."

I'm at the door when Argus taps me on the shoulder and rattles a set of keys Infront of me.

My eyes grow wide when I see them, "Is this a joke?"

"Not at all. Your lovely wife took it upon herself to hunt it down. It's polished and waiting for you."

I am out the door and opening the massive garage door when I see it right in the front, my sexy jag. I know it's not as flashy as other cars I have had or been able to drive but this is my favourite.

This is my first car I got when I passed my licence, the first freedom I ever experienced, and it was given to me from my mum and dad.

The drive is beautiful and seeing Dad's house fills me with great joy. After everything, Adam and Trinity didn't have anything of their own, so I gave them Dad's house.

I know they will never sell it and I know Dad would have been overjoyed to see how much joy they have brought back to the place.

Adam greets me happily and a very pregnant Trin is found wobbling up the hallway to meet me.

"What are you doing? You should be resting."

"Oh, don't you do that to me too. I'm pregnant, not terminally ill. Women for centuries have been giving birth. Back in the day they would give birth in the rice fields, dump the baby on their backs and go right back to work."

I roll my eyes at her for sounding just like Willow, and earning the same jab to my side for rolling my eyes at her.

"If you're done annoying me, what is it you're here for?"

"Actually, I want to see about getting into the vault for something."

Adam looks at me in shock, "but no one left the code behind for it."

"I know. I just want a look I have to at least try."

Adam takes Trin back to relax in the loungeroom while I make my way down to the basement. Once down the stairs, I find the wall I once saw Dad push a certain part and it moved. I find the brick and the small section of it that gives way as the wall opens, revealing a massive volt door behind it.

A loud voice echoes around the basement, "Please identify."

"I am Alexander Harlen."

"Voice recognition confirmed. Please place your hand on the plate Infront of you."

A metal plate opens up revealing a panel with a hand out line. I place my hand in the lines.

"Print identification confirmed. Please provide pin code and retinal scan."

"I don't have the code."

"Please step forward and provide the code and retinal scan."

I step forward as a scanner opens up, scanning my eyes and my necklace.

"Identification complete. Enjoy your day."

The door makes a loud noise as it opens. I step inside, fiddling with the necklace I've never taken off. It's the one thing my dad gave me like his dad did before him and not once did I ever think it held such a closely guarded secret.

The room is filled with everything you could think of from old clothing and paintings to very expensive jewels worth a fortune. I keep walking through the room and notice it must have some self-cleaning thing in here as there is next to no dust in here. The room lights up as I step into each new section until I get to the very back where I see a red velvet curtain.

I push it aside to find several glass cases on stands with not jewels, but simple things like baby teeth, hair, booties, all first-time things from a baby growing up.

These are mine. At the very end in the middle of it all is another glass case with a red velvet pillow, and on it is the dog I made my mother all those years ago.

She kept it and never told me. I open the case and remove the dog. I turn to leave, knocking something to the ground. It's a photo album, *David*.

I flip through the photos and see pictures of him as a baby, of David and Mum together. She looks so happy it warms my heart. Willow thinks about David all the time but just like me we have never been able to handle the fact we never even got to see him in any form.

I look around more and find an urn just like the one we had made for Bonney. It's Davids's ashes, here with all his lost baby teeth and first haircut curls.

I'm startled when I hear footsteps behind me. "Willow."

"Frank never told me how but he did say you had everything you needed to get into this place."

"You knew about all this?"

"Yes, Bonney asked Frank to put some things in here safe and he just happened to let me come with him one time."

"You saw all this?"

"Yes, I cried flipping through all of the pages and spoke to my baby boy but my words and tears were for more than David, they were for all the children I'll never see, for all the women stolen from their families, and for all their children that will never find answers."

Willow has Bonney in her hands. "What made you bring Bonney?"

"I just had a feeling she was needed here today." Willow places the urn with David's while we look around. After a while of rehashing some old history we decide nothing should leave here but decide some day we will bring our own history here to be preserved for the next generation.

Willow goes to take Bonney when I stop her. "She should stay here with all her treasures, but I thought you wanted her on the mantle until you knew what to do with her."

"I know now this is what she would have wanted. All these things are put back here with care and Dad must have felt it meant a great deal to her to allow it. Not to mention, her beloved grandson is here. Why would she leave him here if she didn't think it was the best and safest place for him?"

Willow nods her head in agreement, "But this case isn't big enough for both of them."

"The one that had my dog I made her will be perfect."

We place both urns together and the little dog in front of them. They all fit together so perfectly it's as if they were made to fit. Just as I think that a metal panel opens up at the front of the small pillar that the glass case is mounted on.

Willow gasps as she reaches in and takes out a key and a thin book. On the front it reads, Willow dee Vance/*Loralie Bright*. Willow bursts into tears when she opens the book. Inside are all the babies she bore, their ages, their weight, hair colour, eye colour, sex and the names they were given after adoption and who they were adopted to and for how much.

All in all, I had no idea someone could be kept in constant pregnancy for ten years with two sets of twins and one set of triplets. She has twelve children in total not including Hope, Lyncon, David and the one she is carrying.

If this is the turn out for one of the higher ended girls, I don't want to know how bad it was for the others.

At the back of the book is a handwritten scribble in Bonney's handwriting, 130611, 6124 Bradford Avenue.

"What do you think this is? That's a big safety deposit box key in your hand and that address is one such place. I think that first number is the box that key opens."

In Willow's excitement I am running out of the vault after her. I hear the loud noise of the door sealing shut behind us as I run up the stairs after her. She is out the door and in the driver's side of my jag before I have a chance. I jump in, not wanting to argue with her right now. The determination on her face is incredibly sexy and somehow terrifying.

We are at the address within the hour. Willow pulls out the key, shows the lady at the front and gives her the number that was with it. Without question she gives Willow some paperwork and leads us out the back to a large secure room.

I sit on the edge of the steel table quietly observing my wife. She sits in the chair. The lady returns with several massive boxes that just keep coming.

The room is filled with stacks and stacks of safety deposit boxes. After the final one is laid down, she wipes the sweat from her brow and leaves the room.

Willow twirls the key in her hands for a little while in silent thought of what they all contain. Finally, she opens the first box and inside she finds it filled with documents.

Every one of these holds all the information on all the men, women and children that passed through Bonney's and Victors organizations.

"She saved every single record," Willow says in surprise.

"The police who were on this case should get these documents. Then maybe we can give a happy ending to more than just us."

Willow tears up as I embrace her, "Each one of these is a life. There are so many lives they have ruined."

I run my thumb across her cheek, whipping away her tears. "One phone call and so many lives will be saved."

She gives me a loving smile as I make the call.

Dedication

Dedicated in loving memory of Julie Elizabeth Willetts, loving mother and beloved wife, this story was the last book she read before her life was suddenly cut short, her love of books was only outweighed by the size of her heart.

Darkness fell the day she was taken, the sky wept along with us, a hole left behind that will never be filled, her memory will live on in the countless heart

H.L Jones is a mother of three beautiful children and is married to the love of her life for 16 years, she has an amazing family and incredible friends. By day she works as a community care nurse and by night, a new author who delights in writing fantasy romances and trying her hand at stories with a little more sizzle.

Find me on
Hljonesauthor@hotmail.com
HL Jones| Facebook
hljonesauthor.wixsite.com/website

www.ingramcontent.com/pod-product-compliance
Lightning Source LLC
Chambersburg PA
CBHW020008140726
47904CB00018B/2124